W9-CIK-333

To Bury
the Dead

ALSO BY BRIAN ANDREW LAIRD

Bowman's Line

To Bury the Dead

BRIAN ANDREW LAIRD

St. Martin's Press
New York

A THOMAS DUNNE BOOK.
An imprint of St. Martin's Press.

This is a work of fiction. The characters and events in it are products
of the author's imagination. Any resemblance to humans, living or
dead, is entirely coincidental.

Library of Congress Cataloging-in-Publication Data

Laird, Brian Andrew.
    To bury the dead / Brian Andrew Laird. — 1st ed.
        p.   cm.
    "A Thomas Dunne book."
    ISBN 0-312-15224-8
    I. Title.
  PS3562.A354T6   1997
  813'.54—dc20   96-34916
                                     CIP

First Edition: April 1997

10 9 8 7 6 5 4 3 2 1

For these good women:

Linda Laird
Cynthia Huggins
Wendy Laird
Grandma Laird
Grandma T.

And always
for Wendi
who makes it all
possible.

Acknowledgments

T hanks to Lawrence Clark Powell. Without your generous support this book would not have been written. So you've got that on your conscience.

To my editor, Ruth Cavin—and to Melissa Jacobs, Elisabeth Story, Emily Waanders, and the rest of you at St. Martin's Press.

To my in-laws, the Kulins—Pup, Joe, Marge, and all the rest, with love and affection.

To Lee Sewell, writer and comrade in arms. To Chuck and Cindy McHenry, and of course to Jerry and Eileen, who fed me many times. To Bill and Janet Richards, who give that "sinkhole to the north" some life. To Julie Szekely, for friendship and support.

To Jim Koster, great bookman & arms expert, and Shirley—for advice and encouragement.

To Mary Robinson, librarian and horse-woman. To Sam Smiley, a writer. To Larry McMurtry, for kind words, and to Kathy Allen for the same.

Especially to Gary Paul Nabhan, and to Big Jim Griffith, and Julian Hayden, and Chuck Bowden—and the late Edward Abbey. I urge you to buy all of their books, and read them.

To Bernard Fontana, aka Bunny, a good friend and a fine writer, whose book *Of Earth and Little Rain* I used as a resource for this mystery. And to Stephen Trimble, who wrote a fine book called *The People,* which I have also used as a resource. Also, to Capistran J. Hanlon, for his work on O'odham burials. Any errors are mine.

To Nancy Gullett, sometimes an editor, always a friend. To Norm Keepers, a man of greatness, who kept me on this road.

To Konrad Gatien, a good man, who survives on the far western frontier.

To the great bookpeople of Tucson: Cecil Wellborne and Robert Hershoff, June Martin, Bruce Dinges, Bob Pugh, and Tina, Claire, Marlys and Susan at The Bookstop. To Ron and Elaine Querry. To Gloria Chevars and all my other friends at the Book Mark on Speedway Blvd. in Tucson. To everyone at the Haunted Bookshop. To Ernie Bulow, Buffalo Medicine Books, for early encouragement. To Winn Bundy at the Singing Wind in Benson. And to Sheldon and Richard, my friends at the Mysterious Bookshop West.

To the Meolas, especially my good friend Charlie. To Chris and Jennifer Gould, for many photographs. To Dave Lewis, a tough man. To Joseph Romanov and the Rumps family. To John Munoz and Heather. And to Mike Loghry.

To David and Kathy, and Jessie, and Chris—and to the swarming mass of nieces and nephews, by order of appearance: Kristine, J. Allan, Justine, and Erik. And to Larry Haney and the rest of the family.

To Lorraine Eiler, whose comments improved my work.

To my friends at The Cup, especially Greg McNamee, an early and generous supporter. And to Luis Alberto Urrea, inspired and inspiring writer.

To Bury
the Dead

I am walking in the desert with Ryder Joaquin, just
walking. As we duck under the greedy branches of
mesquite and step through soft sage, he talks quietly,
explaining things to me.
Ryder points at a creosote.
"My mother makes chegai *from that bush," he says.*
I bend down, stick my face in the leaves, inhale the
musky smell.
"It's a kind of tea," he says. "It'll cure headaches,
stomachaches, just about anything. But man, does it
taste bad."
Further on he points at a clump of brush. He sees
movement where I spotted none. I look closer and see
the dusty hump shape of a desert tortoise, clawing its
way through the shade. The ancient, wrinkled
creature moves very slowly, each step a thoughtful
motion.
"Old tortoise," Ryder says, "he really knows how to
move, how to live in this land."
I am walking in the desert with Ryder Joaquin, just
walking. . . .

One

I was almost to Tucson when the body disappeared.

I had taken I-10 east out of Los Angeles, then State 95 south—avoiding the urban madness of Phoenix. At Wellton I got on Interstate 8, a smooth stretch of blacktop that roughly parallels the old Gila River Trail—a path used for hundreds, maybe thousands of years by travelers following the only reliable source of water across the hard and lonely desert between Yuma and Sacaton.

I was driving my Land Cruiser. The boxy old four-wheel drive is of indeterminate color—rust and primer gray over a faded red paint job—but looks aside, it is holding up pretty well for its age. It has neither roof nor doors, and I was sweating in the thin strip of shade provided by its bikini top—a faded piece of black vinyl stretched from roll bar to windshield. It isn't comfortable, but it takes me to the places where the pavement ends and the jeep trails begin, and beyond that to where even those thin tracks fade, and there is only the desert.

And when the world gets to be just a little too much for me—something that seems to be happening more and more often lately—I turn toward the desert. And I walk.

My name is Napoleon. Gray Napoleon. I'm a botanist, which sounds pretty boring to most people. But when you spend your time studying the plant life that grows in the most forbidding environments on the planet, life can get pretty interesting sometimes.

It was June, and the sand radiated heat up to the sere and cloudless sky. The wind came in gusts across the highway, stinging my face and arms. In summer, in the deserts of the Pimería Alta—the shifty region

1

where southern Arizona meets northern Mexico—temperatures can reach 130 degrees by late afternoon, cooling off to 90 or so just before morning. People have gone insane from that heat.

I myself enjoy it. There is something about the harsh, unforgiving eye of the desert that transfixes me, draws me out and away. *Into* it.

At Gila Bend I got on 85, skirting the eastern edge of a vast, empty, hostile piece of desert that the Air Force uses for a bombing range. Abbey said it was the most beautiful place he knew.

I headed southeast at Ajo, weaving a shaky path through the desert on the long leg home, with the bulky rectangular box jutting off the back side.

The body in the box was my friend, Ryder Joaquin.

Was.

Had been.

How, exactly, do you say it when a friend dies?

Ryder was Tohono O'odham. They are the People of the Earth, and their reservation, in southern Arizona hard against the Mexican border, is the second largest in the United States. Only the Navajo reservation is larger.

A couple of years ago, when Ryder was getting ready to move to Los Angeles, he asked me one favor. A promise. If anything happened to him out there, he had to be sure he would make it back. If the unutterable occurred—if he died—he couldn't be left in that strange and terrible place. He had to come home. To the desert.

I pulled into the gas station at Why (good question, it turns out) with the six-foot casket hanging off my Land Cruiser's four-foot bed.

Like Three Points, Why is one of those windblown desert outposts that only exist to meet the dubious demand generated by the junction of two state roads. In this case it is the place where 85 and 86 converge. From Why, 86 veers east toward the reservation, and beyond that to Tucson. 85 drops south to the border. Lukeville. Gringo Pass.

The cars were backed up three to a pump at the station, so I pulled around to the side of the building, by the air and water hoses, intending to check my tires and top off the radiator. The tires were good, and while I waited for the engine to cool I stepped inside the small grocery store, squeezing past the line at the register.

A couple of young vaqueros in dirty straw hats were jawing loudly at each other as they waited, twelve-packs of Budweiser tucked under their arms. In front of them was a seedy looking guy with an I'm-the-next-governor-of-Arizona toupee and a shiny polyester shirt with dark sweat rings from his armpits to his white belt. There were also a couple of quiet men with deep red-brown skin, large flat noses, stocky builds, and relaxed posture who I figured were O'odham, dressed in faded jeans and T-shirts. One had a huge oval belt buckle, shined to a mirror polish. A few other customers wandered through the place, gathering sugary, prepackaged items for imminent consumption—little loaves of death in cellophane shrouds.

I wove my way to the back of the place, ducked into a dark alcove and through the door to the restroom. The *baño* was marginally clean, badly dilapidated, and fresh out of toilet paper. It did, however, have a bar of soap, and running water. I turned on the tap marked "C" and leaned over the sink. The water came out first hot, then lukewarm. Under the summer sun, the desert sand heats all the way down to the pipes, and cold water is something you don't get from a faucet. I scrubbed most of the grime off my face and neck, then dried off with paper towels.

By the time I came back out, the line at the register had thinned. I waited my turn, then paid for fifteen bucks worth of regular. The young woman at the counter was pretty—dark eyes and black hair, beautiful lips and straight clean teeth. I said I would pull around to the pump, and gave her my winning smile. She grimaced. I walked out of the place, letting the screen door slap shut behind me.

And when I crossed around to the Land Cruiser, the box was gone.

If you've ever tried to reconstruct a crowded, confused scene in your head, you know what kind of trouble I was in. The faces had all changed since I got there, and the cars were all different. And I was dumbfounded.

I looked around frantically. A soft wave swept over me, leaving me in a state of mind normally associated with head injuries and mild hallucinogens.

A small man with close-set, brown eyes and leathery brown skin was sitting by the door to the place, his wooden chair tilted back on two legs, resting against the wall. He wore a ratty T-shirt with the words *Van Halen* emblazoned above the faded image of four mop-top rockers. Pulled low on his head was a greasy baseball cap with *Arizona Feed* in an orange and green logo.

His eyes appeared to be closed. I walked over to him and cleared my throat, then tapped him gently on the shoulder. His eyes snapped opened.

"Excuse me," I said.

He looked at my hand reproachfully, then shut his eyes.

"Excuse me," I said again, this time more forcefully. "Did you see anyone around my jeep?" The eyes opened again—deep and brown, the look accusing. He shook his head side to side.

"Didn't see nothin'."

The eyes closed.

I felt dazed. Panic crept up from my stomach. What the hell could have happened? Somebody must have seen it. Who?

If I didn't figure it out quickly, I realized, I probably wouldn't figure it out at all. People come and go at roadside gas stations like rude waiters in a busy restaurant—disappearing around corners, never to be seen again.

My composure was slipping, and I didn't like it. I needed a straight answer. I grabbed the small man's shoulder.

His eyes shot open and his mouth moved as if to protest, but then he saw something, maybe the look in my eyes, and he remained silent.

"I was ripped off," I said. "While I was inside. I'm trying to find out what happened. Did you see *anybody* around the jeep?"

"I told you," he said. "I didn't see nothing." His look was sincere. His hand reached lazily through a hole in Eddie Van Halen's forehead and scratched his tight, brown stomach.

"I was sleeping," he added, with a hurt look.

I let go and rushed inside.

I talked to the girl at the register, a kid pushing a broom across the cement floor. Nothing.

I jerked away and pushed through the door, walking quickly back outside. I stood at the back of the vehicle. Stared at the empty bed. Unbelievable.

Who in the hell would want to steal a body?

Two

The cops who took my statement were bored, hot, and tired. They were from the Ajo substation of the Pima County sheriff's department.

The tall one—rake thin with shiny black hair—asked the questions. The other deputy was short, bald on top with a dark afternoon shadow. He leaned against the trunk of the patrol car, yawning hard every few moments, ignoring me entirely. Finally, as I began repeating my story for the third time, the heat and the lack of commotion stirred him and drove him inside.

"Let me get this straight," the tall one said. The tag over his breast pocket identified him as Deputy Cavroni. "You're reporting a missing person."

"Body," I said again. "A stolen body."

"This *body*," the deputy said. "It was on your person?"

I rolled my eyes. Hot anger started to bubble up inside and I gritted my teeth, willing it away.

"I was taking a body to Tucson. For a funeral. I pulled into the station, went inside to wash up, and when I came out, it was gone."

The deputy nodded, long and slow. He had on his face the look of a man observing a sidewalk shell game—knowing he is being scammed, just watching to figure out how.

"So you were transporting this *alleged* cargo to Tucson, and you left it unattended?"

I stared grimly. Nodded.

"I went inside to use the john," I said.

5

"While you were in the *rest room,* did you notice anything suspicious?"

"No."

"And when you came out . . ."

"And when I came out, the body was gone. Somebody stole it."

He mulled that over, as if it were new information that required thorough consideration. Finally he shook his head and tapped his pen against his little notebook.

"This *deceased individual,*" he said. "Did you have a permit for transport over the state line?"

I stared away glumly for a moment, sighed, slowly shook my head no.

It was turning into a long afternoon.

An hour later, ticket in hand, I was back on the road, heading east, the sun pushing down in great hot waves behind me—a searing white arc light in my rearview mirror.

The bored partner had asked around at the store, talking to the same people I had already talked to, and getting the same general response: Shrug. Scowl. Quien sabe?

Finally, Cavroni had noticed his impotence was showing, so he gave me a ticket—A.R.S. 24–7671, Illegal Interstate Transportation, class two misdemeanor, summons to appear in Ajo Municipal Court on August 7.

I climbed back in the Land Cruiser, shoved the ticket in the glove box, and slammed the lid shut. It sprang back open. I pushed it closed again, more gently, and this time it stayed.

As in so much of the Southwest, the monotony of the roadside between Why and Tucson is broken periodically by white crosses. Some are large, some small, most are wooden, and each marks a place of sudden, violent death—usually by car wreck.

I counted the crosses as I drove—a somewhat morbid habit—and mulled over the events that had led up to my current dilemma.

When it all started I was wandering in the desert southwest of Yuma, looking for stacks of bones.

The bones are from bighorn sheep, piled by O'odham Indians

after the hunt, an ancient custom. From a distance the stacks look like the sulfurous slag piles of long vanished ghost mines. They represent one possible link between the O'odham and the Hohokam—the Ancient Ones—a prehistoric tribe that once lived in the region.

Hundreds of years before the first conquistadors arrived, the Hohokam simply vanished. No one knows why. Some O'odham say that the Hohokam were their ancestors. Anthropologists think that is unlikely. The dispute won't really be put to rest until somebody finds indisputable evidence of a link.

Studying the bone piles, trying to find that connection, gives me an excuse to get out of the city—sleeping fitfully through the unbearably hot days and wandering alone in the empty nights.

I'd been bouncing around the Pinacate for ten days, and I wanted to spend another week out there, but I was low on water and food.

I stopped at a sand-blasted roadside gas station and general store west of Yuma.

The faded sign over the door said "Tuba's." After buying ten gallons of drinking water, and groceries, I walked back outside and used a hose to fill the two large water jugs mounted over the rear-wheel wells.

While the gas pump chugged away on autopilot I decided to call home and check my answering machine. I'm opposed to them in general—answering machines, that is—but they're on the list of things I've come to terms with and accepted. And the older I get, the longer that list grows.

Standing on the wooden porch watching the wind send tumbleweeds skittering across the road and over the dunes—disappearing on secret suicide missions into the desert—I listened to the electronic beep of the machine. I punched in the code and waited while the tape rewound and then played back a string of urgent solicitations from various bill collectors, salesmen, my landlord (saying the rent was overdue), and my on-again-off-again relationship, Maria. We were on again. But that would change if I didn't call her soon.

The last message had been left just a few hours before—a man calling himself Charlie. He said that he was Ryder Joaquin's uncle, and that Ryder had said that I was the person to call if anything ever happened to him. Something had.

I had dialed the number the old man left, charging it to my calling card. Another compromise. They creep up on you.

The number wasn't to a house, as I'd expected, but to the pay phone at a bar called the Top Hat, a stumble-out joint on South Sixth Avenue in Tucson. A confused voice answered on the third ring. Drunken slur. There was some shoving, then a more lucid voice came on. The second voice said Charlie was around, told me to hang on. After a few minutes, Ryder's uncle got on the line.

"You Napoleon?" A touch of suspicion there.

"Yeah," I said. "Gray Napoleon. Your message said Ryder was in some kind of trouble."

"You Ryder's friend?"

"Sure," I said. "Ryder's been real good to me. I owe him a lot."

"Well, I ain't sure how much," he said.

It took some coaxing, but when he was convinced that I was okay, and that he wasn't imposing, Charlie told me that Ryder had died out in L.A. That's how he put it. "Ryder died out in L.A." Just like that.

"Don't really know what happened," Charlie continued. "Only we got a message from my cousin Manny, who's got a phone, and he got a call from someone in L.A. who said Ryder died and somebody better pick up the body soon or it would be too late."

" 'Too late?' "

"I guess they're gonna 'dispose' of him. That's what they said, anyway."

"Oh."

"Ryder said maybe you could do him a favor, if he ever needed one," the voice said. "I guess he needs one. Only now he ain't around to ask."

I drove all night, and in the morning bulled my way through a Los Angeles County bureaucracy that didn't have much use for long-haired, unshaven desert rats who haven't bathed in a couple of weeks.

Finally a little man with rimless glasses and a large cluster of acne on his greasy nose informed me that the Medical Examiner's office could not provide any other information on the case except that it had been ruled a homicide.

"All inquiries as to the details of the case—if any details are *known*—are to be adressed to the detective in charge," the little man said. I opened my mouth to speak, but he anticipated my question. "Detective Furber," he droned, "number's on the file." I wondered how many times a month he made the little speech.

It was a cedar box, nailed shut, with a clear plastic folder taped on top containing a description of the contents: Ryder Joaquin and a few personal possessions. I just signed and wrote down my address and phone number at the bottom. Two big men in light blue jump-suits helped me load the box, lifting it over the tailgate of the Land Cruiser and sliding it forward until it rested against the front seat.

By then it was noon, and when I stopped at a pay phone to call the detective, hoping to get a few details for Ryder's family, he was out. The surly cop who answered the phone did not offer to take a message.

I love L.A.

So I had hit the highway, heading alternately east and then south. Immediate goal, Arizona. Eventual destination, Tucson.

Now, as I thrummed down the road with the four-wheel drive jounc-ing along on its big tires, I mulled things over. Two questions. Why would anyone steal a body—Ryder Joaquin's body? And how was I going to tell his family that I'd lost him?

The first question might be unanswerable. The second was going to be downright painful.

For Ryder's people, fear of the dead is a palpable thing. It can in-vade the senses, affect the mind. When a relative dies, the burial has to be attended to right away. If the dead aren't put to rest, they might grow unhappy on the other side. They might get lonely. Restless. They might decide to come back, and take a few others with them.

For his family, the idea of Ryder's body wandering lost in the vast Sonoran wilderness would be unbearable.

I was thinking that when I realized my problem was even worse than I'd imagined: I didn't even know how to find them. For all that we were friends, I had never been to Ryder's home, never met his fam-ily. We were always going away, constantly in motion.

The conversation with his uncle had been a shock, and in the confusion, I'd forgotten to ask where to take the body when I got back to Tucson.

Where would I find Uncle Charlie? Maybe at the Top Hat.

I decided to stop at home and clean up, then try the bar. Somehow I'd have to track down Charlie, and tell him what I'd done to his nephew. The closer I got to Tucson, the more I dreaded the conversation.

Three

I am standing at the edge of a wide open piece of ground north and west of Gu Oidak, Big Fields. The untilled fields stretch into the distance. Ryder kneels down, scoops up a handful of the earth. He crumbles the dry, gray dirt through his fingers. He looks at me and shakes his head. Then we turn and walk across the field toward the desert in the distance, where there are secrets I cannot imagine.

The sun settled over western hills. Looking out past the scrub and cactus, I understood what Hemingway was talking about. The hills did look like elephants—blue though, not white—giant blue elephants strung together trunk-to-tail and buried to their ears in the desert sand. A long way from where I started, so different from what I once called home.

Life in Madison, Wisconsin, where I grew up in the sixties, was just about the same as in every other American suburb. Barbecues and football and getting drunk 'til you puked at the prom. But there was something on the horizon, something coming. Something big.

Even as a randy high school senior, all loaded up with hormones, with a nose for the too-sweet perfume of a gap-toothed girl named Lisa whose breasts were the most perfect things I had ever seen, I could feel it humming, like a big old freight train in the distance. A thick, powerful, angry vibration.

It exploded two years later when I dropped out of U.C.L.A. just before I was going to flunk all of my classes for the third semester in a row.

I didn't wait for the notice. Like a lot of people, my hold on reality seemed to have slipped away in that first wild year of protest and rebellion, and I stumbled down to the Marine recruiter's office like a man already shell-shocked, looking for a war to claim him. The plug-eared sergeant had just the thing. I volunteered.

I spent three years in Vietnam. For two of them I lived in a bamboo cage sunk in a hole in the ground. To tell you the truth, it's something I don't talk about much anymore.

The Land Cruiser chugged slowly up the steep, twisting road to Gates Pass. A jumbled procession of bicyclists crept along in front of me. The riders panted in the Dutch-oven heat, sweat pouring off their bodies, legs pumping herky-jerky in low gear. I dropped down into second gear and idled up behind them.

At the top of the rise the bikes squeezed together in a bunch where an opening had long ago been blasted through the rock at the tight mountain pass. They spread out again as the blacktop widened, and I pulled around them, crossing over the double yellow to give them some room.

Below, Tucson bristled in the heat. Beyond the urban sprawl lay the mountains—the Santa Catalinas and the Rincons—dark and brooding, black eyes on the stubbled face of the desert.

A thin haze of pollution hung low over the city, reminding me of Los Angeles. That happens more and more these days. Look at Tucson, and think of Southern California. It's not just the flood of urban refugees fleeing their promised land by the thousands. It's all the industry and economic opportunity they're bringing with them. Tucson is booming. It's still a desert town, with a character all its own. And you can still find traces of its historic and cultural heritage if you look hard enough. But it's fading, man, it's fading.

Lately, when I look at Tucson I'm reminded of a line from *Chinatown*. Nicholson leans back in a garden chair and whines to Faye Dunaway, "L.A.'s a small town." That's Tucson. A small town. But it's not going to stay that way.

I eased down the switchbacks out of the Tucson Mountains, bearing right when the road forked, and heading toward the barrio.

My house is an old adobe in a run-down neighborhood south of the business district. At least, it used to be run-down. In the last few years, the neighborhood has suffered the indignity of being "saved." Yuppie entrepreneurs move in and buy the dilapidated houses at

1970s prices, give them the quick fix, flashy restoration, then unload them on overpaid lawyers at heavy profits.

To tell you the truth, I liked it better in the old days. There used to be kids playing in the streets, and families sitting on porches on warm summer evenings. Now there are shiny foreign cars, and houses with bars on the windows. In the old days the neighborhood looked lived-in. And you didn't worry about the moral character of your neighbors.

My place is long and narrow. Wooden floors, walls three feet thick, twelve-foot ceiling. Old adobes are, in my humble estimation, the best desert dwellings ever made. Cool in the summer, warm in the winter. Comfortable and convenient.

My place has no dividing walls inside. It is one long open box, without the usual inconvenience of rooms. The kitchen is at one end, the bed at the other, and between is a living area with a wood burning potbellied stove and a long, comfortable couch. An old claw-foot tub and shower, along with a sink and toilet are against the back wall, the toilet screened off for privacy.

It makes for an unusual lifestyle, but unlike many people, I have nothing to hide from myself.

I don't own many things. Some books, a desk and word processor (on semipermanent loan from the museum), and a few odd pieces of Indian art and desert relics I've picked up over the years, the most prominent of which is a mining cart given to me last year by an old prospector named Archie Blezinger after I did him a favor, helping him recover some stolen property. Archie said he was lightening his load—and the cart was the heaviest thing he owned. It is five feet long and four feet high and solid, rusted iron. It sits right in the middle of the place, and lately I have taken to using it as a laundry hamper— a reaction to Maria's suggestion that I use it as a planter.

The little red light on the message machine was blinking 2. Foolish faithful. Everybody knows a couple of them. The luminous dial on the clock told me it was 7:45 P.M.

I ignored the messages, dropped my keys on the table by the clock, stripped, tossed my dirty clothes into the ore-cart, and climbed in the tub.

I turned on the shower, and let the initial blast of hot water run its course before stepping into the stream. I faced the nozzle, expecting the warm, soft wetness to rain down on me.

What I got was a blast of dark orange gunk that stung as it struck my eyes and cheeks. I jerked away, shaking my head violently side to side. A fairly large particle of unidentifiable brown crud worked its way past eyelashes and under an eyelid. Suddenly I was dealing with temporary blindness and burning pain in my left eye.

I took a step backward, thinking I had plenty of room to maneuver, but rather than hard porcelain my heel came down on something soft and squishy and very slick—the last remains of a once-proud bar of Kiss-My-Face soap.

The rusty gunk from the showerhead, like the urban sprawl of Maricopa County was a gift from the Central Arizona Project. When the powers that be hooked us up and started pumping C.A.P. water into Tucson a while back, they didn't count on the corrosive nature of the heavily filtered, chemically treated water. The city's ancient water pipes have been crumbling ever since. The result is a wildly inconsistent water supply—sometimes clear and faintly bitter, like thinned down formaldehyde, and sometimes foul, dark, and thick, like water from the bottom of a swamp. We used to have great water around here. No longer.

My foot shot out from under me. The shower curtain hangs from an oval rod bolted into the ceiling. I didn't know how much weight the curtain would hold, and I figured that if I latched onto it with my full weight, the whole thing would come tumbling down around me like a slightly moldy polyurethane cape. I twisted as I fell, lunging through the curtain.

I ended up half-in half-out, draped over the tub like a wet towel. My head bounced once on the floor, not too hard, before I caught myself and began to ease down, figuring it would be best to let gravity do the work for me and lower myself to the floor.

That's when the doorbell rang.

I rose slowly, shaking my head in disgust, and reached out to the towel rack, squinting through one eye. As the doorbell rang again, I grabbed a towel from the rack and draped it around my waist. I blinked and rubbed gently at my left eye until I felt the speck of crud shift onto an eyelash. The bell rang again, this time continuing in one long jangle that penetrated my forehead and shook my mind.

"Enough!" I shouted, straightening up and crossing to the door. The towel slipped and I caught it, pulled it tighter. "Enough, goddamnit."

As I neared the door a second noise joined the first. The tinny buzz underscored the doorbell's tyrannous jingle—second fiddle in a hellish duet. Telephone.

Damn, I thought, turning toward the phone, then changing direction again, continuing briskly to the door.

"Ee-goddamn-nough," I growled as I reached the door.

They pushed in hard as I turned the knob.

One was tall and thick, the other short and thicker. That was all I saw before they had me spun around and reeling, tumbling off balance, falling chin first to the floor.

My head snapped back as I landed, and the lights all flickered, then faded to black.

A red light blinking in the darkness. I could see that much. A thin, blurred dot, like the warning light on the underbelly of an airplane. Steady blip on the radar. I tried opening my eyes all the way. The light grew brighter, took on a painful, angular quality. I squeezed my eyes shut, fading back into unconsciousness.

When I awoke the second time, the light was still there. I blinked a couple of times, staring at the beacon in the darkness. It grew brighter, took form, then the number 5 was glaring at me in an angry crimson stare. Disappeared. Glared. Disappeared. The answering machine, I realized.

Then it hit me. Five messages? Hadn't it been on two? Three people called while I was unconsious? How long had I been out?

I groaned, the air escaping my lungs in a low, gravelly noise that sounded very far away. I shook my head gently side to side, then froze as hot pain shrieked through my skull.

I closed my eyes, concentrating on taking deep, slow breaths. After a few minutes the pain eased. My vision was still cloudy. I blinked a few times, clearing my eyes, and gently touched my chin with the fingertips of one hand. Feeling for damage—cuts, abrasions, dried blood. None. But a lump had formed on one side of the cleft, and the skin felt tight and swollen.

I tried moving again, sat up slowly. It went over better this time. I rubbed gently at my neck. I was achy and stiff, and my ears were ringing softly, but otherwise I seemed okay.

My apartment was another story. It had taken a beating. Everything that had been up was down. My clothes had been dragged from the dresser, the drawers thrown on the floor, the cabinets in the kitchen area were strewn about as well. My desk was overturned, emptied, one leg broken.

Apparently every shelf in the place had been cleared, every movable object lifted, turned upside down.

Finally my eyes wandered back to the clock and the answering machine. They had been on an end table by the bed. Now they were on the floor, the message machine upside down. I moved sluggishly through the haze to where they were, picked them up, righted the table, and set them back in place. As I did this the 5 turned into a 2, and a minor feeling of relief washed over me. The clock said it was 9:35 P.M.

For a few minutes I stumbled around, picking things up, straightening the mess. I tried to figure out what was missing. Apparently nothing. What the hell was going on? First the body disappears, then a couple of clowns break in and trash the place, but don't steal anything. Had the world gone absolutely ape-shit?

I thought about calling the cops. But remembering the way things had gone at Why, I decided against it. It wasn't worth the trouble. They'd probably just give me a ticket: A.R.S. 75–9618, Disorderly Living Space.

What to do?

I looked down. The towel was still wrapped around my waist, hanging loosely from my hips. I walked carefully, softly to the shower. It was running. The water was clear.

I took a lukewarm shower, dressed, and went looking for Uncle Charlie.

Four

The small man appeared suddenly, his face leering into mine.

I was northwest of Tucson, near the rez. Nobody at the Top Hat knew where Charlie was—or if they did, wouldn't admit to it. So I figured the best place to start looking for him was out by the rez. I'd just pulled into the parking lot of the only business open at 11:30 on a weeknight. The red neon sign on the roof of the bar said "Nacho's."

The small man leaned toward me, his exhalations like little vaporous explosions in my face. I pulled away, trying to escape the smell of his noxious panting.

"Ehp you?" he said.

"What?"

"Uht?" he mimicked brightly. Then he chuckled, clearly pleased with himself. "Uht? Uht?!" he repeated. He leaned further in, his eyes dancing in crazed, confrontational glee.

I climbed out of the vehicle, easing past him. The small man jumped back.

"Ehy!" he said. Then, "Ehy!" again, feeling it out. "Ehy, ehy, ehy," he settled on the new word, his eyes gleaming with watery happiness.

I walked across the dirty parking lot toward the building. Pickup trucks, both old and new, were parked nose-first against the wall of the building. Fords, Chevys, GMCs, many beaten and battered by the wind, the sand, the desert. Like the building itself, they were ugly but functional. The new ones were a different story. Their paint jobs were clean, waxed, shining deeply in the moonlight, their spotless windshields reflecting the lights of the building in distorted ovals.

As I reached for the door to the bar I felt a tug at my shirtsleeve. When I turned, the small man was at my elbow, his bleary eyes and stubbled face screwed down in an expression of anxiety.

"Ehy!" he said. Then he grabbed my elbow in a frail grip, like the claw of a parakeet. "Ehp you?"

I pulled my arm away from his trembling fingers. Ehp you? I thought, confused. Elp you? Then I understood.

"Maybe," I said. "Maybe you can. You know where I can find a guy named Charlie Joaquin?"

A look of intense concentration filled his face. His eyes grew clear and dark like twin sand rubies. Then his knees locked and his eyes rolled up into the sockets, the lids flapping down. He wavered for a moment, and I thought maybe he was going to fall over backward. I moved forward, ready to grab him by the shirt if he went down, ease him to the dirt. But his eyes shot open and he stared straight at me.

"Ain't no Cha'lie awquin," he said.

"No?" I said.

He shook his head deliberately.

"Well," I said, "whether there is or not, I've got to find him." He mulled that over, and I turned away. With my hand on the door to the bar, I stopped and looked back.

"Do you know Ryder Joaquin?" I said.

Suddenly his eyes were hooded, his look suspicious.

"Ryduh awquin's did."

"Yeah," I said. "Ryder Joaquin is dead."

The small man backed away from me, fading into the darkness. For a moment I thought about following him. If he knew about Ryder he must know the family. I could press him for information. Grill him. Whatever the hell it is they do in the movies. But he was already shuffling around the corner of the building. Gone.

I pushed past the heavy wooden door, and stepped into the darkness of the bar.

The bartender was tall, a thin man with dark skin, pale eyes, and hair so gray it was nearly silver. It seemed, in fact, to shimmer above him like some kind of insane, glow-in-the-dark hair-helmet. After a moment he worked his way down to where I sat at the end of the bar.

18

He stood there looking at me, his eyebrows fixed in a questioning arch. In the background, country music whined from the jukebox.

"Modelo," I said. He turned, dipped into a dilapidated, stainless steel cooler that had long since quit reflecting the dim light of the bar and was rusting through at one end. He pulled out a bottle, popped the top with the opener hanging on a string from one of his belt loops, and slid it across the bar to me. Then he reached down and grabbed a mug, adding it as an afterthought.

I lifted the bottle to my lips, sucked down some, then set it next to the mug. He turned to walk back down the bar, but I caught his attention.

"Shot of tequila, too," I said. He poured a shot and set it down. I nodded. "One for yourself," I said. When he'd poured himself the drink and was about to raise it, I spoke again.

"Looking for a man named Charlie Joaquin," I said. The bartender just stared. "I'm a friend of Ryder," I continued. He slowly set his drink back on the bar in front of him, untouched. "Anyway, I need to get in touch with Charlie."

The bartender raised his eyebrows, then lowered them in a dark squint.

"Four dollars," he said, pushing the tequila across the bar toward me. I paid him and he walked away without another word.

I did both shots and raised the beer, chasing them with a gulp. Then I slowly spun my bar stool around and leaned back, both elbows resting on the cracked vinyl padding of the bar, and looked around the place.

Well, Napoleon, that was cool, I thought. Now you're getting somewhere.

At the end of the bar, three dark-skinned men—probably O'odham—sat talking quietly, huge shoulders hunched close together. They leaned over their beers protectively. One looked vaguely familiar, but I couldn't figure out from where. Maybe one of the times I traveled the rez with Ryder. Maybe my imagination. I stared too long and the one nearest me looked up, gazing at me hard from under dark eyebrows. I looked away.

A couple of vaqueros were playing pool at the table, clomping around in their boots, leaning jauntily against their sticks between turns.

19

The booths were mostly empty. But against the far wall two couples crowded together in one of them. Smoke floating up from their cigarettes, they talked loudly, occasionally bursting out in laughter that drowned out the scratchy sound of the jukebox.

Every fourth or fifth song one of the women would slide out of the booth and weave over to feed the juke.

I faced the bar again, and began nursing my beer. I listened to all of Waylon and most of Willie, and I still hadn't figured out how I was going to get from this place to Ryder's family.

Obviously, the O'odham guys were my best bet. They might know where Ryder's family lived. They looked to be about Ryder's age. The age he would be, I reminded myself grimly. One of them might have known him.

But approaching them, getting them to talk to me was another thing entirely.

I am a short, scrappy white guy, with blue eyes and dirty blond hair that needs cutting about five minutes after I leave the barber. My clothes are scuffed and tattered—faded jeans, old T-shirts, and worn-out combat boots. I look like what I am—an ex-hippie who has perhaps made not quite as much of his life as his parents wanted, the kind of lonely desert refuse that nobody misses when it's gone. And most of the time that's just how I feel.

Nobody out here would mess with me as long as I kept to myself. But it might be different if I started asking the wrong questions. It's a delicate thing, and I've dealt with it before, doing research. Then, of course, I was only looking for plants and stories, not the relatives of a dead man. There's plenty of distrust for outsiders on the rez. With good reason. It's close to the border, and it's out in the middle of nowhere. A person, like a body, can disappear awfully easy out there.

I finished my beer and swung back around to the bar, tried to catch the bartender's eye for another.

That's when the door to the place whooshed open and the bikers stumbled in.

They were big and trashy, in dirty jeans and black leather. One of them wore a hat with "Arizona Militia" across the front. Three guys, with a woman walking in the middle. She was cackling at the presumably hysterical comment one of them had just made. Her head was tilted back, mouth gaping open, and her crooked, tobacco-stained teeth looked like the twisted tines of a rusted rake. Her long, blond hair was black at the roots, and she flipped it over her shoulder as she leaned back to give one of the guys a goose. This elicited another comment and more of the grating laughter.

I hunched low over my empty beer bottle, watching them in the dirty mirror behind the bar.

Two of the guys were just plain big—six feet and change, pushing two hundred pounds. The other one, he was tremendous. Maybe six-five, two eighty, a long, thick beard with strands of gray, belly like a wrecking ball.

They paused and looked around the place. Their gaze landed on me, and the woman stretched up and whispered something funny in the big man's ear. His laugh was jarring: a disconcerting, high-pitched squeal, like helium squeaking out of a balloon—eeh-eeh-eeeeh.

My eyes widened. The blonde whispered in his ear again. He glanced up and caught me watching in the mirror. I looked down, but it was too late.

They spread around me, the two of them on my left, the big man on my right, the woman in the background. I didn't say anything, just hunched a little lower.

I could feel the old trembling in my stomach, the panicked, manic spark flickering, wanting to grow, the flame to spread. I looked inward, controlled it.

"That your gray turd out front?" the big man said.

I didn't answer, squinted at the shimmering image in the mirror, then turned partway toward him with a look on my face that I calculated to approximate total, disenfranchised stupidity.

"What?"

"The jeep," the big man said. "The jeep yours?"

I nodded slowly.

"Your idea of a joke?" he said, and now there was force in his voice, a deep trembling, like water above an earthquake, portending darker things below. The other two moved in closer. There was something about these three—the way they moved, fluidly, gracefully, despite their weight—and the look in their eyes, like the cold dead stare of sand sharks, that told me they were serious trouble.

"Joke?"

21

"What are you, a parrot? Yeah, that bumper sticker, is that some kind of joke?"

I felt that anger start trembling again, deep inside, moving upward. I felt the hair stand up on my neck, my elbows draw back reflexively. Hold it, I told myself, hold it down.

"Bumper sticker?" I said with a look conveying complete ignorance. Total moron. True idiot. Brain dead patient.

The big man growled in frustration. "I'm talking about the gray jeep," he said in a strained voice, "the four-wheel drive with the bumper sticker on the back."

Of course, I knew what he was talking about. The sticker, in red, white, and blue lettering, said "Fuck the I.N.S."

The I.N.S. is the Immigration and Naturalization Service—the goons who patrol the border.

I thought about educating my new friends, sharing a few tidbits with them—like the rising number of people killed by Border Patrol agents, and how few trials there are for those killings. And how there is a growing trend in the international community to regard our Border Patrol as being not much different from the death squads in Central America. After all, they do virtually the same things: roam in cover of darkness, shoot to kill, answer to no one.

I wanted to tell this motorhead about a woman I met in Mexico whose son made the mistake of taking a one-night job from a local coyote. All he had to do was be a mule for a couple of hours, carry a backpack through a gaping wound in the fence along the border, cross an open field of desert scrub, walk down into a canyon and follow a nearly invisible trail for a few miles. He and his companions would meet a truck and be relieved of their burdens. For this work he would receive one hundred American dollars. Enough to feed his family for a month.

The group was less than a mile north of the border when a voice shouted from the darkness, telling them not to move.

"Migra!" someone yelled, and the mules began a frantic scramble back toward the fence. All except this particular young man. He dropped his pack and raised his hands in the air, as ordered. The Border Patrol agent who eventually reported the "incident" and two of the mules testified to it in court—all he did was stop dead still, sling off his backpack, and put his hands straight up in the air. For that he was shot in the head.

The agent who shot him spent an hour hiding the body and covering his tracks. Then he turned to his partner and said, "I don't think anybody else has to die tonight. Do you?"

When the story finally got out, prosecutors in Tucson gave in to pressure from human rights organizations, mounted a halfhearted investigation, and made a less-than-adequate effort to bring the agent to trial. The case was thrown out of court by a good-old-boy judge named Mitchum. Insufficient evidence to warrant a trial by jury, he said. Mitchum, of course, was a former Border Patrol agent himself. So he knew about these things.

I felt like telling the barber's nightmare in front of me that therein lies the basic rub—you give a bunch of undertrained, high-testosterone nutcases an arsenal of heavy weapons and four-wheel-drive vehicles, and you let them roam unchecked along the line, killing without fear of reprisal, you're headed for trouble. Which is what we seem to be getting more and more of every day.

Before I could say anything, the goon spoke again.

"What you got against the Border Patrol?" he said. Before I could answer he continued. "My father's Border Patrol. My brother, too." His goon friends moved in closer, glowering at me omnivorously.

At the other end of the bar, the vaqueros had stopped their game, and the couples were looking around blearily from the booth. The Indians had stopped talking and were watching with half-closed eyes. Except for the tinny whine of the jukebox, the bar was quiet.

"The yellow-haired lady was buried at sunset," Willie sang, "the stranger went free, of course . . ."

I estimated my chances of making it out the door, slamming it shut behind me, and running for the Land Cruiser, starting it and peeling out before they stomped me into squishy little pieces with their steel-toed boots. Zero. Less than, maybe.

"Shithead," the big man said, putting a hand on my shoulder.

"Well," I said, ignoring the nickname. "Yeah, kind of a joke."

I looked down at his hand and wished I hadn't. His fingers were like greasy rolls of quarters, and at the tip of each roll was a little pit of open, angry flesh where the nails had been chewed away.

The big man looked down at his hand, realized I was staring at it, and jerked it away. He actually seemed embarrassed.

"Some kind of joke," he said, slapping my back and digging his hand into my shirt.

The feeling rose again, like an electric coil in my stomach, heating, rising to my throat. I felt the hand lift me off the stool. I tried to swallow the rage, choke it down. I didn't want to fall into the trap, didn't want to give in to the fear, the anger.

But then he was spinning me around, and the center was breaking free—fiery gyre—and the world was a whirlwind. A voice inside spoke clearly in the maelstrom. It told me I had one chance. Take down the big man—fast—and put a little space between me and the other two.

He had hold of my left shoulder and was pulling me toward him. My right hand was free for one strike. Neck or eyes? Eyes are good. Without them most men are finished. But temporarily blinded, a big man will sometimes grapple instinctively, pull you tighter. The key is area. There is a certain area, close around a big man, within which your odds of prevailing at, or even surviving personal combat diminish precipitously. I needed to create space, and merely blinding the big man with a split-fingered hand strike to the eyes would not do that.

I went for the throat, coming around hard, swinging from the shoulder, pistoning at the elbow, up on my toes for the follow-through.

It almost worked. I caught the big man flush, a square shot with a hard fist, under the chin and above the collar. He emitted a startled gurgling noise and let go of my shirt, falling to his knees on the cement floor.

The problem was the other two. They were between me and the door. And rather than being thrown off balance by the attack, they were spurred to motion. Together they bore down on me, driving me back against the bar.

I didn't fight the momentum. Instead I fell back with them, concentrating on the one on my left, measuring him up, getting a sense of where he was, where he would be.

I pivoted on my left heel, snapped my right leg upward, lunging with the knee. Unfortunately, the blow landed on his thigh, missing

24

the more-centered target, slowing him not in the least. He was going to have a real bad charley horse, though.

Then they were pushing me down under their combined weight, my shoulders banging against the bottom of the bar stools. No way to get leverage. My arms were caught above my shoulders, and I wrapped them around my head as the blows started raining down.

It didn't look like I was going to get another opening, and I had begun to consider the possibility that I might die from internal injuries right there on the floor of the bar when the big guy caught his breath and unwittingly gave me a second chance.

He plunged in and pulled the other two off of me.

"Mine!" he yelled at them, "mine!"

His huge, hairy face grinned down at me, an overgrown Heat Miser in a twisted Christmas tale. He grabbed the front of my shirt, and I let him lift me, saving what I could, trying to gather strength, dropping my arms down and back, coiling.

As he pulled me full upright, I reached out and grabbed his shirt. He pulled back one clenched fist, cocking the arm all the way back to his shoulder, readying to come around with a blow like a thrown hammer. His face glowed and his eyes shone with rage and joy. Joy and rage.

I pulled forward and stomped down on his right foot in one quick, hard motion. A look of surprised pain washed over his face. I stomped on the foot again.

His shoulders went limp and his head snapped back. His face rose in a high-pitched howl.

I punched him in the throat, cutting the howl short.

Given a second chance, I wasn't going to repeat my mistake. As the big man went down, I pushed off him, sending him into the other two. I lunged straight ahead, going over them in a high-stepping motion, and headed for the door.

Almost made it. I was reaching for the handle with my right hand when the weight hit my shoulders. It was either elbows or a heavy chair. I couldn't tell which. But it hit me solidly and I went down hard. Then I felt something, probably a boot, drive into my side. And another.

I pushed to my hands and knees, reached out with my left hand for the door handle. Tried to drag myself up. Pressed down on the thumb latch and felt the suck of cool air, then something went "pop" on the back of my head, and my vision turned into a field of black with little white dots zooming around in it like bacteria under a microscope.

Then I fell to the floor unconscious for the second time that evening.

Five

I awoke staring at the small man's upside-down face. I closed my eyes and spun in the blackness for a while.

When I opened my eyes again, the face was rightside up, grinning over me like a gap-toothed clown from a child's nightmare. A thick piece of spittle had formed at the center of his lower lip, and as he opened his mouth to speak I watched the clear, viscous liquid make the inevitable leap into oblivion—floating, floating, then landing on my shirt.

"Ehp you?" he said.

I groaned. He grinned. I shook my head gently side to side, tried to smile back. Failed. His grin grew wider.

I sat up slowly, felt another groan, long and low, escape my mouth.

He helped me to my vehicle, bearing a surprising amount of my weight on his skinny shoulders.

I sat in the Land Cruiser, sideways on the bucket seat, feet on the running board. After a while the pain ebbed. I twisted the rearview mirror around and checked my face. Not bad. A little dirty. Ugly. But they hadn't beaten me to a pulp after I went out. Mostly I ached around the ribs and stomach. I had taken a couple of hard blows to the midsection, and might be pissing blood for a few days. And as I felt through my hair for hidden damage, I realized I was going to have a big lump on the back of my head.

I looked at the small man, who stood by the front fender with an expectant look on his face. I shrugged. He smiled.

I scanned the parking lot. No motorcycles. The three O'odham men from the end of the bar were standing around the bed of a pickup, talking quietly. They didn't seem to notice me. My attention returned to the small man.

"I'm trying to find Charlie Joaquin," I said carefully. "I need to talk to Ryder's family."

The small man shook his head. "Ryduh's dead."

"I know. Listen, I'm not a cop, and I don't work for the state. I'm a friend of Ryder's. I was supposed to bring him back for the funeral."

I explained about the body disappearing, and how I was looking for Uncle Charlie so I could tell the family what had happened.

When I was finished the small man smiled and nodded gently. Then he explained, with his crooked tongue, where I'd gone wrong.

It turned out, Ryder's uncle was his mother's brother. Charlie Reyes. Uncle Charlie. The small man said that Charlie and Ryder's mother and the rest of the family were out at their house, south of Kitt Peak, down a long dirt road beyond Baboquivari. Near Santa Rita Village.

Hard to find. Especially at night. He could show me. But how's 'bout a beer first.

I shook my head no.

"A beer after," I said.

He paused, reflecting seriously for a moment, then he nodded his head agreeably.

"But isn't it a little late?" I said. "Won't they be sleeping?"

The small man shook his head no. His expression was grim.

"Eh gettin' ready fuh a funeral."

Six

From Nacho's we drove west past Kitt Peak; then, ignoring a No Trespassing sign, turned south, passing over a cattle guard onto a bumpy dirt road. We passed an empty stock tank, and drove through a small open area crisscrossed with tire tracks and littered with shards of glass from what looked to be thousands of broken beer bottles. Then the road narrowed, and we began climbing up and down a harrowing series of rocky hills.

On our left, Kitt Peak was a massive wall of darkness. Above, the white domes of the observatory shimmered like distant hunchbacked ghosts.

I dropped the Land Cruiser into first, then shifted to two-wheel low, and finally stopped and climbed out, walked around the front, and locked the hubs for four-wheel drive. The road became a jagged, spine-jarring succession of holes and rocks.

We crept along until we came to a fork. The small man pointed left, toward the black mountain. It rose against the night sky like a tremendous, elongated anvil set hard in the desert floor. The O'odham call it Baboquivari, which describes it in their language. For them, it is the center of the universe.

After Earth Medicine Man made the world, and First Born sang his song, the sky came down and met the earth. That's when Elder Brother, I'itoi came forth. He was the Life Giver—and while Coyote and Buzzard worked on their own creations, I'itoi made man. Like all gods, he molded his work from clay. When he was done, he made the Crimson Evening—the haunting soft red light of the sunset reflected by the mountains. He gave the Crimson Evening to the People, and told them to stay in this place, and live here forever—this land, he said, is the center of all things. Then he went to his home among the high cliffs of the dark mountain, and he has rarely returned since.

The small man was quiet. When we came to the second fork he pointed left again.

"Maybe," he added.

In my headlights, the pitted, rock-strewn road looked like the surface of the moon. I was beginning to worry about the damage one of the big rocks could do if I misjudged a dip or a rise and came down hard on one. We were ten miles from the main road and thirty-five from the nearest phone. A long walk if we broke down.

I braked to a stop.

"Maybe?" I asked.

"This is the way," he said.

"Maybe."

"This is the way," he said.

I ground the Land Cruiser into gear and continued on.

We crept down the jeep trail, eventually working our way around the southwest end of Baboquivari to a place where the road smoothed out. In a few minutes we were pulling up to a low adobe structure. The smell of beef and beans wafted across the warm night air from the cookfire under the ramada. This was the Joaquins' home, or ki as the O'odham say it.

I stopped, switched off the headlights and climbed out, and was walking toward the ki when a tall woman, whose skin beneath her golden tan was every bit as white as my own, came marching out of the darkness, her aquiline nose tilted up regally, and began barking questions.

"Who are you and what do you want?" she asked. She spoke with a heavy accent—French, I decided without too much trouble.

She was thin, with long brown hair tied back tight, and big brown eyes. Her jaw was set in a challenging clench, her lips full, painted with slick lipstick that shimmered in the moonlight.

In her tight blue jeans and a crisp white linen shirt she seemed out of place among the dust and the cactus—a city girl who had dressed her casual best but wasn't ready for the stiff formality of the saguaros, the dry wit of the desert. Standing in front of a crumbling adobe house, she was an anachronism.

A ramada had been constructed against one wall of the house, wooden poles planted in the desert floor, holding up a thatch roof. A fire burned in a pit under the ramada, and three O'odham women bustled quietly around the pots of food cooking there.

"What's the matter," she said, "cat got your tongue?"

I looked back over my shoulder for the small man, but he'd kept his seat in the Land Cruiser. Apparently, he figured he'd done his job getting me here.

If here was here.

"I'm looking for someone," I said.

"For who?"

"A friend of mine . . . that is," I stumbled, tried again. "Ryder Joaquin—"

"Ryder is dead," she said, her voice dropping to a hiss. "What do you want? Who are you?"

Her eyes burned. Even in the darkness they glowed as if from an inner light. A bright, hot fire back inside there somewhere, just waiting to be fanned, to spread. The look was a strange mixture of anger and defiance. Then, as I held her gaze, I noticed the bottom lip quivering a little, as if she were hiding something behind the bold façade. Fear, I thought. Pain.

It was a look I'd seen before, a face I'd stared into too many times, too many years ago, in a place I'd tried to leave behind. It was the face of one who has seen too much, one who has had people close to them die before their eyes and has not been able to digest that fact. And it keeps rising like emotional bile to the surface of the consciousness before it is forced down, to be dealt with later . . . but later never comes. You just keep forcing it down again and again, until it stops coming so frequently. Then one day you realize it hasn't been there for a long time—so long you don't remember the last time you were aware of it—and you feel sick and scared, and ashamed, but also . . . relieved. Because you know it can't happen again. Until the next time.

"I was a friend of Ryder's," I said.

"You were his friend?" a new voice sang sweetly, quietly from the darkness, and a new face emerged into the light.

The old woman was short and thick. Her skin was dark, her hair silver with the faintest streaks of black.

I nodded. Then, realizing she couldn't see me in the darkness, I said, "Yes," and added, "I'm Gray Napoleon."

"Come," she said, "come into the light, where I can see you." She had hold of my sleeve and was pulling me along toward the house.

"Juan," she said, and a young man appeared from the darkness at the edge of the ramada as if he had been waiting for her to call. "Wake up your uncle. Tell him the man is here." Then she turned to me again. "You'll want to talk to Charlie."

"I suppose I will," I said. "But I'm afraid I have bad news."

"Not now," she said. "No bad news yet. First, Charlie. Then news, bad or good. It's sometimes one, sometimes the other. I never try to guess."

I followed her into the house, the French woman right behind.

It was a two-room building with open windows. Inside, a lantern flickered on a table, painting the room with its sickly yellow glow. Black smoke leaked up from the lantern toward the roof.

An old army cot was set up against the back wall, and a huge man lay on it, his back to the room, snoring loudly, his jeans and T-shirt separating to reveal the large brown expanse of his flat hips.

The boy shook the old man's shoulder gently, whispered in his ear.

The old man rolled over and sat up slowly. He pulled his shirt down over his large belly, rubbed his eyes with the palms of his hands, and sat there with a faraway look in his eyes.

The old woman pulled out a chair and motioned me to sit, then she dropped down into the one opposite. The French woman hesitated, looking at the old woman. The old woman nodded and the French woman sat.

I looked around the room. The floor was dirt, obviously sprinkled with water and swept often, so that now it looked so hard and glassy, it could have been mistaken for a single sheet of dark tile. Besides the chair and the cot, there was a low end table in one corner with candles and bread, framed pictures and red flowers. A shrine to the virgin.

At the far end of the room was another door, this one covered by a thick cotton blanket.

The man on the cot shook his head, then squinted at us through the lantern light.

"Man," he said. "Was I ever asleep."

I nodded and smiled. He scowled. He breathed heavily and leaned back against the crumbling adobe wall. His eyes were tired, and it looked like he was going back to sleep. The old woman watched him, then turned to me. In the lamplight I could see that her dark skin was seamed with wrinkles. She cleared her throat.

"I am Theresa Joaquin," she said.

I don't know why I was surprised. I had never met any of Ryder's family, but the resemblance was obvious, the curve of the nose, the brightness of the eyes.

"Ryder's mother?" I said.

She nodded quietly, and looked down at the scarred tabletop. She ran her finger back and forth over a long, black mark that looked like a cigarette burn.

"I'm sorry," I said, then faltered. "I, I just don't know what. . . ." Now it was my turn to stare at the table.

"Ryder told us all about you, Mr. Napoleon," she said.

The man on the cot grunted.

"This is Ryder's uncle," she continued. "Are you awake now, Charlie?"

"I been awake."

"Ryder said you were a very important man," Theresa Joaquin said.

Again, Uncle Charlie grunted. This time I noted a definite negative tone.

"He said you were a man who listened to our people, respected Tohono O'odham, respected our land. He said you were a man the white people listened to, who they also respected."

"Ryder was a good man," I said. "A good friend. I owe him a lot."

"You helped in the lawsuit," Uncle Charlie said.

"A little," I nodded. "As much as I could."

"But maybe the lawsuit didn't make much difference. Maybe the ground's still drying up, and no one can live on the rez."

I didn't have an answer for that.

"He has done what he can," Theresa Joaquin said. "We owe him for that."

Again Uncle Charlie grunted.

"We were making coffee," Theresa Joaquin said. "You want coffee?"

"Sure," I said, leaning back and sighing. "Coffee would be great."

Theresa Joaquin rose and went back outside. I heard her talking with the women under the ramada. They spoke in O'odham, and their words were soft and scratchy, like warm wool rubbed gently against your ears.

As she walked back, she paused outside the doorway, looking over at the Land Cruiser. She came in with two cups of coffee. She gave one to Uncle Charlie, and one to me. She went back out, then returned with another cup, which she handed to the girl.

The cups were chipped and cracked, mismatched but serviceable, the kind you can buy for a dime apiece at the Salvation Army Store. The coffee was hot, milky, and very sweet.

"That lawsuit," Uncle Charlie said. "The judge told them they couldn't take no more of our water without paying for it. But it didn't matter. They kept taking it anyhow, some way. So then they said they would start paying for it. But we haven't seen any money." He made a noise of disgust and shook his head.

"Maybe another lawsuit," I said. "What about the council lawyers?"

"Naw," he said. "They're just in on it."

"If it went to court again, you would speak up like you did before?" Theresa Joaquin asked.

"I'd be there," I said. "And I'd tell the truth, just like the first time."

She nodded at that.

"It's settled then," she said. Again she looked out in the direction of the Land Cruiser. "But you said you had news."

"After I talked to Uncle Charlie," I said, "I drove straight out to Los Angeles—"

The French girl had been quiet, but now she interrupted, her voice rising sharply, her eyes flashing.

"You are the one?" She turned to Theresa Joaquin. "He is the one who is bringing Ryder? This is the man?"

The old woman nodded.

"Where is he?" the French girl demanded. "Where is Ryder?"

Ryder's mother and uncle watched her quietly, then looked at me. They waited quietly for my answer.

I drew a deep breath. Let it out slowly. Nodded.

"I'm the one. I was already halfway there, so I went to get Ryder and bring him back. But . . . something happened."

I turned to Theresa Joaquin.

"I'm sorry," I said, "and I just don't know how to say it, but Ryder disappeared."

The French woman exploded. "Disappeared! How is this? How does this happen that one disappears?"

Again I shook my head.

She turned to Ryder's relatives. "I do not believe him. He does not tell the truth! What have you done with Ryder?"

"I didn't *do* anything." I said, feeling the heat rise on my neck as my composure began to slip away. "Something happened."

Uncle Charlie was sitting back now, his head cocked to one side, arms crossed on his chest, his eyebrows raised incredulously. I drew another deep breath, and leaned forward. I felt the pain around my midsection, winced. I rested my elbows on the table and rubbed my temples. I was tired. God, I was tired. Until that moment I hadn't realized how badly I needed rest. When was the last time I slept? I tried to track it down. In the desert, before Los Angeles, before the phone call. Could that have been just two nights before? It seemed longer ago than that.

"You need more coffee?" Theresa Joaquin asked.

"Not now," I said. "Maybe after."

Then I told her about the highway, and the heat, and Los Angeles, and how I had lost her son's body.

When I was done they were all quiet. Then the French girl stood and faced me.

"This is outrageous! Such lies!" She looked around at Ryder's family for support. "This could not happen, you see? He is lying!"

"Excuse me," I said, "but who are you?"

35

"Why do you ask this, who am I?"

"Well, I don't know you, and you don't know me, and I'm kind of tired of listening to you call me a liar."

Uncle Charlie grinned at that, and Theresa Joaquin looked away. If there was a disagreement between the white people, we were going to have to work it out between ourselves. The French woman looked around the room, with that fire in her eyes, then I saw her face change, soften, and she sat down.

"My name is Caroline Cheanne," she said. "I am friend of Ryder's. We live together in Los Angeles." Her voice softened. "I have had a very hard time. If I have said rudely it is because of this."

"Okay," I said. "If that's a French apology, I prefer the kisses. But let's move on. If you lived with Ryder in Los Angeles, how did you end up here?"

"Three months ago I leave Los Angeles to go home. My mother is very old and I had not been back to France in many years. At first I go for one month. But my mother is sick, so I stay two months, then three. All this time, I do not hear from Ryder. I send him postcards each week. Each week I watch the mail, but nothing.

"I telephone. At first I get the machine and I leave messages. Never he calls me back. Then I call and the line is disconnected—perhaps the bill has not been paid.

"One week ago, I return to Los Angeles. I think, perhaps Ryder will be at the airport. But he is not there. I take the taxi to my apartment—it is a long way, and very expensive.

"In the apartment there is a note from Ryder. It says he has gone home—to Arizona. It tells me to follow him as soon as I can.

"I drive from Los Angeles. My car quit to work, how do you say—it broke down. And then I had to get rides. I hitchhike. I hitchhike all the way to Tucson. I am checked into a hotel downtown. But Ryder's note—it tells me to come here, to the reservation, where his family lives. So I am hitchhiking again, and I go to the tribal headquarters at Sells this evening, and they find me a ride here.

"And then they tell me . . . they tell me—" Her bottom lip began to quiver. She clenched her jaw and bit back the tears. If they were ever there. "—they tell me Ryder is dead. He is not meeting me. Only there will be a funeral. Not Ryder. Only a funeral."

The room was quiet. I thought I heard the crunch of gravel under tires outside. I looked out the doorway, and after a second a pickup crept around a corner of the dirt road, and pulled to a stop behind my vehicle. For lights it had only the orange glow of parking lights.

Theresa Joaquin rose from the table and walked out to the truck. She stood at the window for a moment, apparently engaged in conversation with the driver. As my eyes adjusted, I could just make out the silhouettes in the cab—two or three large-shouldered men.

After a moment, Theresa turned away, and the truck pulled slowly away, disappearing down the road to the south. A few hundred yards from the house its lights snapped on, and it sped up a little, bouncing down the dirt jeep trail.

When she returned, Theresa Joaquin was carrying a battered metal pot. She poured coffee into the cups, then took the pot away. No one spoke until she had returned to her seat without a word about the visitors.

"Now what shall I do?" the French girl asked.

I felt my lips twist up in a crooked grin.

"Why do you look at me with this . . . this . . . smirk?!" She pronounced it *smuhk*. "You do not think that Ryder would be friends with someone like me? Who are you to regard me this way, to look on me with this . . . contempt?"

"It's not that," I said. "It's just that you just seem so out of place here."

Theresa Joaquin and Uncle Charlie looked her over carefully, as if weighing that statement.

"But I do not *feel* out of place. And I did not feel out of place with Ryder. If he were here he would not let you talk to me this way."

That got me, and I was quiet for a moment.

"I'm sorry," I said finally. "It's late. I guess you're not the only one who's tired."

Uncle Charlie ran a hand through his hair and yawned.

"Know I am," he said.

"We are all tired," Theresa Joaquin said. Then she turned to me. "We had been preparing for the funeral. But now there is not going to be one."

There wasn't any anger in her voice; it was not an accusation. It was just a reckoning of how things were, told with a sad kind of acceptance.

"We should not have been preparing for the funeral before you brought my son home," she said. "It is bad luck to pretend you know what's going to happen. It is bad luck to expect things."

"It's my fault," I said, "I wish there was something I could do."

"Maybe you done enough," Uncle Charlie said. Theresa shushed him.

"Maybe you can help," she said. "Maybe you can find my son, and bring him home?" She offered it as a question to which she did not know the answer, rather than a request.

"He's not gonna find nothin'." Uncle Charlie said.

"Maybe yes, maybe no," Theresa Joaquin said. "You know anyone else who's going to help us? You want to call the police? You—a man who knows what they can do himself? You think they'll help you find Ryder?"

She had a point.

Charlie just shook his head and stared at the ground.

"I really don't know what I could do," I said.

Theresa Joaquin looked at me plainly for a moment, then nodded. I felt the guilt welling up inside. I tried to convince myself that I wasn't just saying it, there really *was* nothing I could do. Cops don't care for my kind any more than they do for the Uncle Charlies of the world. If I got in the way of something they were investigating, they would take me out, or go right through me, without so much as a flash of the lights or a blast of the siren. And if as I expected, the vast, impenetrable legal bureaucracy was not interested in the case, nothing I could do would change its brain-dead mind.

Still, I owed Ryder. I didn't have the slightest clue who would steal his body, or why, and there was probably no way I could have prevented it. But no one could say for sure, and I was just left with his family—and they needed my help. I told him I wouldn't leave him out there. I told him I'd bring him home.

"I'll ask around, see if I can find anything," I said. "The sheriff's deputies in Why took a report, and I can keep on them, see if they make any progress."

"You do that," Theresa Joaquin said. "And you come tell me what you find out. Maybe you'll find Ryder, then you can bring him home. Maybe not. It's best not to hope for too much."

"I'll remember that," I said. "It might help if I knew what happened to him in Los Angeles. Did you get any letters or phone calls?"

She shook her head.

"No letters," Uncle Charlie said. "But he did call one time over at the Top Hat. I wasn't there. That was a while ago, two months, maybe three. He left a message with Joe—that's the bartender—said he'd call back again. But he never did."

"What about his friend? Have you heard anything from Sandy Asoza?"

"Ain't heard nothin'," Charlie said.

"Nothing," Theresa Joaquin agreed.

"Well, it'd probably be a big help to talk to him. Is there any way you could find out if he's still in L.A.? Or, if he's left there, where he went?"

"If he came back, we'd have heard," Theresa Joaquin said. "His mother lives in Quijotoa." I recognized the O'odham name for the village we gringos call Covered Wells. "And sometimes I go there to visit my sister," she continued. "Maybe I could go visit sometime soon, and ask about Sandy."

"It would be helpful if you could get a phone number . . . some way to reach him.

She nodded thoughtfully. I dug in my pockets for a piece of paper and a pencil, scribbled down my phone number and handed it to her.

"Call me there, anytime."

"Thank you," Theresa Joaquin said. "I believe what Ryder said about you, I believe you'll help us if you can."

I smiled, turned, started to walk away.

"Wait!" It was the French girl. She had remained oddly silent through the last part of the conversation. Now her demanding voice followed me through the darkness. "I must to go also."

Much as I disliked the idea of a long drive back to the city with her, I figured she could tell me what Ryder had been up to in Los Angeles—at least until three months ago. And anyway, looking at his family, I knew I'd done enough to make their lives miserable. I couldn't stick them with her. I grimaced.

"You can come . . . and you can tell me all about L.A. But I have another passenger," I said as we neared the Land Cruiser. "You ride in back."

Seven

*I climb out of the Land Cruiser and shake off the
dust, then follow Ryder toward the church. It is dusk.
Along one wall of the dirt courtyard stands a row of
tall saguaros with stumpy arms. Like strange
crowns—halos in a rusted Christmas pageant—
small iron crosses perch atop each saguaro, twenty,
thirty feet above the ground.
I follow Ryder into the church. Inside it has been
painted to look like an O'odham basket. We sit quietly until long after the sun has set.*

I dropped the small man back at Nacho's. The bar was closed, the
parking lot empty, but he insisted on being let off there. I stuffed a
five-dollar bill into his outstretched hand.

"Thanks," I said.

"Okay," he hopped nimbly out.

"Vaya con dios," I said.

"Seguro."

Then he disappeared in the darkness.

"You want, you can ride up here now," I said to the French girl.
She slid into the bucket seat, and I pulled out onto the dark, empty
highway, heading for the distant lights of Avra Valley, and beyond
that Tucson.

"Where are you staying?"

"I am at the, oooh, I do not remember." She paused for a moment.
"It is the . . . Hotel Senate! Yes?"

"No." As far as I knew there was no Hotel Senate in Tucson.

"Congress?" I asked. "The Congress Hotel?"

"Ah, yes, this is the one."

I nodded, turning my attention to the road.

I was quiet for a few minutes, thinking she might start the conversation on her own. But she stayed silent, sitting back in the passenger seat, the warm desert wind blowing against her face and tugging little strands of hair loose from the tie at the back of her head, whipping them around her forehead.

It became apparent that she had no intention of speaking. Finally, I broke the silence.

"I was just thinking," I said.

"Yes?"

"About Ryder," I said. "We had some good times."

"Oh." She turned away, looking out over the emptiness of the blackened desert.

We were east of Three Points, still a few miles out of Tucson. To the north, the lights of Avra Valley blinked like a thick spread of Christmas tree lights.

A few years back, that valley was dark and still at night. Nothing but the silence of the saguaros, a few mobile homes, the Desert Museum, and the movie location turned tourist attraction called Old Tucson. But every year a few more lights blink on out there. And now, there are plans for—surprise—a hotel and housing development. The slow cancer of civilization.

It's the same everywhere. The Verde Valley is overrun and Sedona is one big strip mall—golf courses, retirement communities, and tourist traps. The Navajo Nation is thriving, and cities are popping up like mushrooms in the once wide-open emptiness up north.

Such a fragile land, this western desert. One or two voices rose up against the flood of humanity as the gates were opened. Voices crying from the wilderness. But the tide has been let slip; there is no going back, no return to virginity.

When I got back from Vietnam it was like my blood had been drained and replaced with a slow-working acid. I was burning from the inside out. I can't describe it any better than that. It felt like every bit of bodily fluid, every tissue was on fire, and my head pounded as the bitter fluid raged through it.

My Lai was in the headlines and people were talking about war crimes. The war was almost over for everyone who hadn't been there. But for some, it seemed like it would never end.

I stayed in Madison for one day and one night, got up early the next morning, before sunrise, quietly packed some clothes, and headed west. One hundred years too late.

It was familiar territory, the American West. Throughout my childhood the old man took us touring for a few weeks every summer in the National Parks and Forests beyond the hundredth meridian, camping and reveling in the vast open spaces. At night, gathered around a cement picnic table, or on the ground around a campfire, he read to us from the works of Thoreau and Audubon, Stegner and Guthrie. We explored Monument Valley and Bryce, Zion, the Petrified Forest, Death Valley, the Redwoods, and the Olympic Peninsula. It was my father's one great legacy. He would leave us little else, but these places we were damn well going to know and understand. Some day, he said, you may learn to love it.

I was going back there to escape a world, a place, an existence I never wanted to have known. Perhaps the high cool places could chill the Southeast Asian fire inside. Or maybe the deserts of Chihuahua, Sonora, and Mojave would push the heat higher, bring it to a final boil. In any case I needed to go. Out there. Away.

What I found was another trap. More rage. The West was long closed and I found myself in a land that was being eaten alive.

Industry had sunk its deep roots, and was growing like tumbleweed. The mining companies were piercing, sucking, and masticating the Earth's mantle. Tourism was a cancer. And everywhere there were roads. Highways and interstates, interchanges, bridges and thruways, business loops and scenic routes. Roads, roads, and more roads. More roads meant more people, and it was easy to see where that was leading.

It seemed hopeless. What could you do?

Then in '75 Abbey came out with the *Monkey Wrench Gang*. A little while later I hooked up with Dave Foreman and a few other likeminded anarchists. Earth First! rose to the war cry.

Here, finally, I had a just cause—a war that, though it might be as unwinnable as Vietnam, was at least understandable, at least *right*. And an outlet for the anger. The anger was always there, just below the surface, hot and vibrating in a barely controlled rumble, like that train on the horizon all those years before.

We cut power lines and spiked trees. We sabotaged tractors and road graders and back hoes. We used any means available to slow the destruction of the last of the wilderness.

To tell you the truth, I'm not sure we did a damn bit of good. When the FBI finally sent their little maggot in to break up the group, Dave and a few others took the fall. I was one of the lucky ones who slipped off into the darkness.

I lay low for a couple of years, spent some time working the fishing boats in Alaska.

And when I finally made it back down to the desert, I found the rage had eased.

I stumbled into a job at the Desert Museum—the sprawling desert menagerie west of Tucson—and took a couple of botany classes at the university.

A year later I got serious. I'd finally found something I could sink my teeth into without feeling the urge to tear it apart. Studying the plants—not just looking at them under the microscope and learning the Latin, but getting to know their properties, the folklore surrounding them, the way the different biotic communities interrelate—grabbed hold of my mind and forced my unflagging attention. Learning the traditions of the people of the desert—their foods and cures and building materials—was a remedy for what ailed me. And pretty soon it seemed like the rage had disappeared completely.

I earned one degree, then another. And that was enough. With an M.S. and a few papers published in journals and magazines I found something I never dreamed existed: a job that took me out there. A legitimate excuse for going away, into the wilderness.

I work for the botanical wing of the museum. They provide me with a little cubbyhole they call my office, and enough money to live on, almost. And they don't expect too much from me in return. No set hours. No long-term strings. Occasionally I provide the research material for a new exhibit, and when they need it I'll write a page or two or ten describing the wonders of the Sonoran desert for a publicity pamphlet. In the summer, things slow down and I'm pretty much on my own. Mostly, I wander the desert and meet people whose cultures stretch back thousands of years. I study their ways of agriculture and plant use, their lore and their customs. Then I write it all down. And I wander on.

But lately I get a creeping feeling, a sense of impending crisis. And I wonder, where will we walk away to, when there's no more "out there" out there?

I looked at the French girl—Caroline. I wondered if she would care about any of it if I told her. It didn't really matter. What did matter was any information she had that might help me find Ryder's body.

"How did you meet Ryder?" I asked.

I glanced over at her. Met with an icy glare.

"What about Sandy, did you ever meet him?"

"No," she said.

This wasn't going anywhere.

"Look," I said. "I don't like this any more than you do. And I can see where maybe you wouldn't be inclined to trust me. But we both knew Ryder, we were both his friends. You saw how his mother was, saw the look in her eye, didn't you?"

She didn't respond, but I glanced over again and saw that her look had thawed a little, so I stumbled on.

"I told her I'd help her, and I'm going to do just that, with or without your cooperation. Ryder . . . Ryder was a good friend. I met him at a time when my life could have gone a couple of different ways, neither of them very good. He opened up a whole new direction for me. So I owe him.

"His mother—I don't think she's going to sleep very well until I find him and bring him home. Tell you the truth I really don't know how to do that. But I know I have to try. So if you don't like me, don't trust me, don't want to talk to me, that's something I'll learn to live with, but for Ryder's sake, for his family's sake, you ought to start giving a shit."

I thought it was a beautiful speech.

"I loved him," she said, and when I looked over I saw real emotion, saw the depth of the loss in her face. In the faint glow of the starlight, her chiseled features turned suddenly haggard, ragged, taut.

"I loved him in my way, and he loved me in his way. We—how do you say—we gave it a shot."

I nodded.

"But it wasn't good. It never worked, really. We felt so much for each other. He was so good, you know, deep inside, all the way down. Ryder was good. Not like most people. And I loved him and tried to be with him, but somehow, we . . . missed the crossing."

I watched the road as she spoke, stealing a glance at her now and then. She stared straight out the window, her eyes focused up and away, like someone in a trance. Now the muscles of her face had relaxed and she betrayed no more emotion.

We passed Kinney Road, and a couple of cars merged with us. The highway spread out into four lanes, two to a side, divided by a wide and shallow arroyo where clumps of Indian ricegrass shimmered, silver-white in the headlights. I kept to the right, letting the faster vehicles pass.

"I did not say this to his mother, because I like her very much, and because I truly loved Ryder, but when I returned to France, it was because we were no more."

"You'd broken up?"

"Yes," she nodded. "Many months ago. We had broken up, and then I went home. I was in very much pain. It was a hard time. I hoped the time apart would help us to get back together. Sometimes to be apart is to love. But when Ryder did not answer my letters, did not return my phone calls, I felt it was truly over between us.

"Then, he sends me a letter asking me to return, saying he needs for me to be with him."

"He asked you to come back?"

"Oui, yes. So I come back to California. But he is not there. Only a note saying he has gone home. I followed, and I find that he . . . he is gone. And I do not know why, I do not know what happened while I was away, but I feel like part of me is gone. I feel deeply . . . the regret."

We were both quiet for a while.

Then I said, "I'm sorry."

It kind of choked up on the way out and ended up sounding lame, but I decided not to try again. Everything in its time.

"No," she said. "I am the one sorry. I am simply so very tired. Perhaps now I can rest, then later we can talk."

I felt her eyes on me.

I nodded, and she sat back again, letting the warm, dry air scrub her face clean of the world's ugliness.

Soon we were in Tucson. I headed downtown. The streets were mostly deserted and shortly we were pulling into the cramped parking lot of her hotel.

The Congress Hotel sits on a tight, triangular block downtown, across from the railroad station. It is a squat, two-story building—a virtual skyscraper when it was built right after the turn of the century. That wasn't long after the Earp days and the gunfight at the O.K. Corral in Tombstone. In fact, on a visit to Tucson in 1882, the Earps gunned down Frank Stilwell on the railroad tracks just a couple of blocks west of the hotel. The tourism industry had nowhere to go but up.

Now the Congress rests in the shadow of downtown Tucson's ever taller, ever blander skyline.

In addition to rooms, the hotel has a low-rent bar, a thumping pulsing pounding dance club for the black raincoat crowd, and a cafe. The coffee is lousy, but the food is superb.

I parked by the big, glass double-doors to the lobby, and walked with the French girl to the desk. The clerk handed her a key, and a message on a pink slip of paper. She read the message without emotion, then turned to me.

"Perhaps you would walk with me just to my room? It has been a long night, and I am still upset."

I hesitated.

"Do you have a photograph of Ryder?" she asked.

"No."

"In my room," she said, "I think I have one, pretty—how do you say—recent?"

I nodded.

"Come on," she said, "I get it for you."

I walked with her up the steep flight of stairs, and followed her down the hallway to a room at the east end of the building. She opened the door and I followed her in. The room was clean and old-fashioned—like opening a door back in time to 1940. The bed sagged, and the carpet was threadbare, but the windows looked out on the old west university neighborhood, and in the distance the blinking red lights of the radio towers were visible atop the Catalina mountains.

I felt a strange, throbbing at my feet—the music from the club below, vibrating through the floor.

"Would you mind," she said, "to turn on the lights."

I walked into the room and one by one found the switches and flicked them on. I looked around, shrugged.

"And the bathroom?"

I turned that light on as well, and poked my head into the shower. Empty.

When I came out of the bathroom she had moved around to the other side of the small, sagging bed and was leaning against the wall.

I stood there awkwardly for a moment.

"No one in there," I said at last, indicating the bathroom with a thumb.

She nodded.

Again the awkward pause, then, "You were going to give me a photo," I reminded her.

"It is late," she said, "and I do not remember now where I have it."

"Oh." What was her game? She had asked me up here, the photograph had been her idea.

"Listen," I said, taking a step in her direction.

She moved farther away, keeping her back against the wall, the bed between the two of us. Her eyes were hooded now, and dark.

Suddenly I felt very aware of my situation and my surroundings— alone in a hotel room with a strange woman—and wasn't all that comfortable.

I figured she must have felt the same way.

"Here," I said, digging in my pockets for pencil and paper. I jotted down my phone number and put it on the dresser as I went out. "That's my number. Call me tomorrow. I'll buy you a bad cup of coffee."

Eight

Even as I turned the knob, I got that prickly sensation at the back of my neck. Don't ask me how I knew. Maybe the deadbolt wasn't twisted all the way home, maybe the porch light had been turned on in my absence, maybe it was simply something in the air as I pushed the door open. To tell you the truth I didn't examine it all that carefully, I just knew, with absolute certainty, that somebody was in there. Waiting.

I thought about backing out, getting in the Land Cruiser and taking off. I'd met enough new people for one day.

But where would I go? Finally I said to hell with it.

"Why haven't you called me?" she asked. "Where have you been? What happened to this place, what's going on? Are you okay?"

I was used to this. Her mind moved at three times the speed of light and only slowed down when she was asleep. And sometimes I wondered if then . . .

Maria Kazhe is the best lawyer I know. The only one I've ever known well, but you don't have to take my word for it. Her reputation is well-established.

She is Apache, born and raised on the San Carlos reservation. Her parents ran a trading post up north on Highway 70.

She knew, she says, from the time she was four years old what she was going to be. Lying on the floor in the back of the store, reading every Perry Mason novel Erle Stanley Gardner ever wrote, she received her calling.

When she told her mother at the start of the eighth grade what she was going to be someday, the woman just nodded, and said, "Okay, then you gotta do good at school. Starting today. You gotta do better than everyone else."

For Maria that came easy, and at seventeen she was accepted to Arizona State University on a full academic scholarship. She spent the next four years going to school full time, living in a girl's dorm.

In the middle of her junior year, her father died of a heart attack. She went home for the funeral, and told her mother she had decided to return home and help with the store. Her mother put her on the next bus back to Tempe. Two months later the old woman died in her sleep. Again Maria returned for the funeral. It was arranged for her brothers to take over the business, and the next year Maria graduated at the top of her class.

Four years after that she graduated from the University of Arizona College of Law. She achieved the highest score in the state on her bar exam, and then started the long struggle to establish herself as a lawyer in southern Arizona. The deck was stacked against her in the male-dominated profession, but in the law game, verdicts are the great equalizer, and Maria did not lose a case in her first ten years as a trial lawyer.

Her cases included a couple of unpopular, seemingly unwinnable lawsuits against local corporate entities—the biggest of which was a government-contracted missile manufacturer whose pollutants were poisoning groundwater near the rez, causing cancer rates in the area to triple. The all-white jury not only ruled in favor of the plantiffs, it awarded three times the amount Maria asked for in damages.

I met her through a friend of a friend when I needed a lawyer after the FBI busted Earth First! I was broke. She gave me free legal advice. Since I hadn't been named in the indictment, she said, I should probably lay low for a while, not worry too much about it—and maybe consider changing my tactics, try reflecting on what I wanted to do, and how best to do it.

That's when I headed north. And over the next few years I did do a lot of thinking. I'm not sure I ever came to any conclusions. But when I returned to the desert, I was a different man.

When I got back to Tucson, I looked her up and thanked her for helping me. She asked if I'd taken her advice. "Some of it," I said, "some of it."

49

At first I was intimidated just looking at her. She is five-eight, but walks five-eleven. Piercing brown eyes. Black hair. Skin like none other I've touched—like the darkest, deepest sunset, like the richest iron-filled earth. But her beauty is the least of her attributes. In court, she is a shark among sharks—a great white, swimming restlessly through the legal ocean. And I know that I am not the only one who is so affected by her presence. Prosecutors give her plenty of room. It is intimidating to know that the person you are with could eat you in one bite.

When she asked me out, I was surprised. But also attracted. One thing led to another, one day to the next.

Her voice was coming through the darkness from the far side of the room. After locking the door, I worked my way carefully in that direction.

"I haven't had the chance. I'm fine. And as to what's going on," I said, trying to tick off the questions one by one in my head, "I have no idea."

"Three out of four," she said sleepily, "I assume you don't know what happened to this place either?"

"Actually," I said. "Two thugs happened to this place. But I have no idea who they were."

I found the bed in the darkness, pulled my clothes off, and climbed under the covers.

"So?" she said.

"I will tell you all about it," I said, "tomorrow morning."

"It'll have to be tomorrow night. I'm in court early."

"What time?"

"I'll be out of here at six."

"Ungh." I started to crawl back out of bed to set the alarm.

"I brought my own," she said.

I flopped back to the mattress.

I lay on my back, eyes closed, instantly at the edge of sleep. After a moment I was pulled back to consciousness by something. Her gaze. I opened my eyes and looked at her.

"Go to sleep," she said softly.

And before my head had sunk all the way back to the pillow, I did.

Nine

In the dream, I was running through the desert in the night, running so hard it could not possibly be a dream. Arms pumping, lungs screaming, heart pounding. But not just from exertion. There was something else. Something deeper. Fear.

Branches of palo verde and mesquite lashed out of the darkness, clawing at my clothing and scratching the exposed skin of my arms and neck as I plunged past.

I fell with a thud in the soft sand of an arroyo, ended up on my back, staring at the sky. The stars spun slowly around some distant point parallel to me.

Dark clouds appeared, roiling quickly across the stars. The clouds were so dark, so heavy. Rain clouds.

The monsoons!

The clouds piled in the sky, blotting out the light of the moon and stars, and I was filled again with the strange, creeping fear.

Then I heard the noise. Coming from somewhere behind me on the trail. A muted, animal cry.

I lunged at the bank of the wash, and tried to pull myself up, but the rocks and dirt crumbled underfoot, and I slipped back to the sand.

The noise broke out of the darkness, closer now.

A bolt of lightning flashed, illuminating the wash in stark contrast. Thunder followed with a crash.

Splat. A raindrop hit the back of one hand, then—splat—my arm. Then the sky broke open and the water came down.

Again I tried to scramble up the bank, but now it was mud, and I was slipping, sliding in the darkness.

Another bolt of lightning, and the noise, back there in the desert, rising to a steady, empty howl. Close. So close.

I glanced over my shoulder but still couldn't see anything.

The wall of mud in front of me began to tremble. I backed away, wanting to turn and run, but the sand was so soft under my feet that I could hardly move. The ground shook harder, as if some forgotten god was under there forcing its hand through to the earth's surface. Then the thick, gnarled root of a huge mesquite pushed out of mud, uncurling down the bank of the wash.

The noise came again, almost on top of me, the groan rattling through me like the afterblast of a sonic boom.

I reached out and touched the root. It went stiff against the wash bank. I grabbed hold and pulled myself hand over hand up out of the wash.

I was standing beneath the limbs of a monstrous mesquite—larger than any I'd ever seen. The pods like lumpy bananas, the beans like smooth walnuts.

I wanted to stop and examine this thing—this rarity. It was clearly an incredible new species. *Prosopis giganteus.* I patted my pockets for notebook and pencil. Nothing.

A piece of paper skittered across the ground, dodging raindrops. The wind flicked it up and took it away. I ran, following it into the darkness.

The earth was shaken by a series of quick, hard, percussions—blam-blam-blam, straight in a row.

The howling grew louder. It was above and behind me now, almost at my ear, incredibly loud, and another series of explosions.

I looked up, saw the shadow, terribly low, felt the wash of jet engines, the streak of the rounds, and the dark oblong shells, then they hit the ground with fiery explosions.

Blam-blam-blam.

Well, I thought, this is getting ridiculous. I rolled over and pushed myself up from the pillow. The dream faded as reality stuck its ugly face in mine.

The knocking came again.

Ugly and loud.

Blam-blam-blam.

I rolled my legs over the side of the futon, stood up, and pulled my jeans on. I groaned softly as I walked to the door, feeling a deep ache in my ribs.

I reached for the knob, then thought better of it, remembering the last uninvited visitors I'd had.

"Who is it?"

"Open up, Napoleon," a reedy voice came from the other side.

"Who is it?" I said again, as I backed away from the door, and dug through some of the mess by the couch, looking for an appropriate object.

"Police, Napoleon, open the door or we come in anyway."

"I'm taking a shower," I called, rusty railroad spike in hand. "Just leave the flowers on the porch."

"One last time, Napoleon. You open it, or we break it down."

"Well, when you put it like that . . ." I placed the thick, metal spike carefully on the floor an inch from the door, and braced it with my foot. Instant doorstop.

I twisted the deadbolt.

"It's unlocked," I said, leaning one shoulder against the door, further to support it if they tried to push through. "Open it slowly and put your badge up where I can see it."

The knob twisted; the door came open an inch and a half, and stopped against the spike.

I peered around. Muzzle to muzzle with a semiautomatic handgun.

"That enough badge for you?" the voice asked. "Now open the goddamn door, before I open you."

"Yeah," I said, backing away slowly.

He pushed against the door, but it was jammed against the railroad spike. For a moment I was filled with indecision. I looked around the room. The windows are all high up in my place, ten feet from the floor, running in a row near the ceiling. There is a back door. But I figured if the voice behind the gun, the man behind the voice, was really serious about using the weapon, I would be dead by the time I got halfway across the room.

"I said open it, Napoleon. Now!" The voice rose quickly into a petulant whine—the sound of mindless, childish rage.

53

"Yeah," I said, "sure, okay, step back and I kick this thing out of the way, and you come in. No problem."

"Now!"

I pushed the door closed quickly but gently, moved the spike to the side, and stepped back.

The way they burst through the door brought back memories, but this time I was prepared, and I'd retreated all the way to the middle of the room by the time they got past the threshold.

The first one was short—five-five, one-sixty—and he had the gun. He was dressed in neatly pressed gray slacks and a blue cotton shirt, buttoned prissily to the throat. The outlines of his white, short-sleeve undershirt showed through. He had gray hair and pale eyes, and he wore glasses with conservative silver frames.

He was also the one with the petulant voice, and as he stepped into the room, he pointed the gun at my chest.

"Good morning, darling," he said.

The sloppy man came in behind him. He was big, maybe three hundred pounds, and six-two or better. His hair was curly and dark, with touches of silver. A thick black stubble covered his jaw. His rumpled, khaki pants were spotted here and there with dark stains—a big yellow splotch of what looked to be mustard had splattered against his right thigh and dried there. His shirt was some kind of Hawaiian print, missing a button at the bottom, and open at the neck. Deep rings of sweat ran under his arms, and sweat glistened on his forehead and chin, giving his face a greasy sheen.

"Or to be exact," he said, "Good day. I trust you slept well?"

I didn't have an answer for that. My attention was taken up entirely by the gun in the short man's hand. He backed me farther into the room. I stumbled over something, fell backward, landed hard. The short man smiled.

"It's like this," he said. "Yesterday we paid you a visit, but you didn't know where your manners were, and you ignored us the whole time we were here."

"To be exact," the sloppy one said, "You didn't even say hello."

"Right," the short man agreed. "So we figured we'd come back— see if your manners improved—if they haven't, maybe teach you a little lesson."

"A lesson in humility," the other one said.

"Humility . . . and *manners,*" the short man said. "So what do you say, want to talk?"

"To be exact," the sloppy one added, "are you prepared to answer our questions?"

"Anything you say," I replied without taking my eyes off the gun.

At first I'd thought it was a .45, but when he shifted his hand I noticed there wasn't any hammer, and I realized it was a Glock—nine millimeter automatic. I felt sweat break out at my armpits.

"I'll answer any question you want to ask, but could you please just point that thing down a little bit? Say, at my knee or my foot?"

"I'll take care of this," he said, raising the gun so that it was aimed at my face. "You just do what we tell you."

"Right." Sweat was breaking out on my forehead now, and I reached up very slowly with one hand and wiped it away. The short man smiled again.

"We have reason to believe," the sloppy one said, "that you recently had a . . . delivery problem. And it is our job to elicit from you the facts involved in that unpleasant—"

"What we want to know" the short man interrupted, "is where's the body?"

"Body?"

He racked the slide on the pistol and aimed it again at my forehead. It would now take only a few pounds of pressure on the trigger—the barest flick of a fingertip—to blow most of my head into chunks.

"Oh, the body. To tell you the truth, I wish I knew."

"Why not," the sloppy one said, "tell us what you mean by that?"

Then, sitting on the floor, propped up on my elbows, with the nine millimeter pointed at my right eye, I recounted for them what had happened on the way back from Los Angeles, leaving Ryder's family and my trip to the rez the night before out of it.

When I was done, they moved away from me, and spoke quietly for a minute or two. It was obvious they were debating, but I couldn't make out the words. Finally the short man got all red in the face and his voice climbed.

"Yes, yes, yes," he said.

But the sloppy one just shook his head calmly back and forth, and continued pressing his case quietly. Finally the short man gave up.

"Fine," he said, "it's your decision."

The sloppy one turned to me.

"Would you mind getting dressed?" he said. "We're going for a ride."

Ten

The old man sat hunched over his desk, studying a weathered piece of paper. He had not looked up since I entered, and I was beginning to get the uneasy feeling that he had forgotten I was there.

A few minutes before, I had arrived with my new friends. After hustling me into my clothes, the two goons had walked me out to the street—one in front, one behind. A shiny new Jeep Cherokee—deep blue, with big tires and dark tinted windows—was parked two doors down.

The short man motioned me to the passenger side and opened the door for me. The sloppy one sat directly behind me, and the short man crossed around to the driver's seat.

We drove up Fourth Avenue. A big old freight train was rumbling along the tracks at Broadway. The short man turned right, and we dropped down through the underpass, the train roaring above us. We headed east, then north, and soon we were making our way up Campbell Avenue, toward the mountains.

We followed the narrow, winding road into the foothills, then turned off on a long brick driveway. We wound our way up the red brick road toward a house visible in the distance at the hilltop.

To call it a house amounted to extraordinary understatement. It was a villa, a mansion—it was spectacular. Long and low, with dark granite walls and windows the size of swimming pools; it could have been a museum. Because Frank Lloyd Wright had designed it, and because the most powerful man in the city owned it, and perhaps also because it sat high on a hill against the Catalina Mountains, where it could be seen from miles below, it was instantly recognizable.

I had seen it on the covers of slick magazines celebrating the scenic beauty of Arizona and the wonders of better homes and cactus gardens—the kind of magazines you find in the dentist's office, the ones nobody ever steals.

The articles always spoke glowingly of the Wright design, and the wondrous furnishings inside. And always, there was one name associated with the architectural marvel—a name bigger even than Wright. A name that meant influence and prestige and money. This was the home of Torrance Power.

The front door was opened by a tall, thin man in a dark suit. He did not introduce himself.

"This is the one," the short man said, then he and the sloppy one walked back toward the Cherokee.

The thin man led me down a long, dark hallway. The floor of the hallway was done in huge Mexican saltillo tiles—shiny, six-foot squares of baked orange clay—and our feet clopped like horses' hooves as we walked. The walls were illuminated by the intermittent glow of small lamps aimed at ornately framed paintings—multicolored rectangles in the darkness.

Some of the artists I recognized, others I couldn't place. The ones I knew were big guns—huge in western American art circles. There was a sweeping Maynard Dixon panorama of horses on a desert plain. A charge of cavalrymen by Remington. An unusual early work by DeGrazia of a mining camp in Northern Sonora. I paused to gape at a Frank McCarthy, and when I looked up, the thin man was at the end of the hall, waiting. My gaze returned to the paintings—easily a million dollars' worth, I figured, and that was just the ones I could identify.

I shook my head and quickly caught up to the thin man. He led me through a patio to a large open room and left me there. The north wall of the room was glass—an unbroken view of the cliffs along the southern slope of the Catalinas.

I sat in a boxy wooden chair—wide arms, green leather cushions—and waited, taking in the view, staring up at the mountains.

After a few minutes the thin man reappeared.

"Dr. Power will see you now," he said. Then he directed me

through another door and down another hallway, this one hung with rugs. Most of them looked to be Navajo, and very old.

At the end of the hall was another door—dark, ancient-looking wood. The thin man tapped lightly, then pushed it open and indicated a chair for me. He stood there next to me, looking across the desk at an old man, as if awaiting further instructions. Power said nothing, nor did he look up. After a moment the thin man turned and walked out of the room, silently pulling the door closed behind him, leaving me to wonder if the old man had communicated with him telepathically.

The old man was short and spare. He stood on the far side of the desk, a thick, comfortable-looking high-backed chair pushed out behind him. When he was young, I thought, he would have been wiry.

His hands were lean and delicate, and they did not shake at all—the hands of a pianist or a surgeon—with only the lightly liver-spotted flesh clinging loosely to bone to indicate that they were not the hands of a young man. His shoulders curved a bit, as if tugged down by the weight of time, or maybe just his suitcoat.

His most amazing feature, though, was his head. It was a great, curving orb, a luminous bulb above his shoulders. The cranium was tremendous, broad and high, the thin hair having retreated almost entirely to the sides and the back, as if surrendering ground to the power of the intellect there.

The eyes were sharp—an intense brown, like the glint of sunlight on oiled walnut, and the mustache was cropped very close to the upper lip.

In his time, I figured, he must have been a lady-killer. He had the kind of quiet power that seems to feed off of sexual energy—like the young Howard Hughes, or Gatsby incarnate.

His reputation, of course, was nearly equal to either of those characters. It was said that Tori Power owned more of Arizona than anyone except the state and federal governments. By today's standards his fortune was old—California money descended from an empire of orange groves and newspapers.

He'd moved to Tucson in the sixties, and bought most of it in the next ten years. He owned bank buildings and malls, agribusinesses and politicians. And land—lots of land.

"Mr. Napoleon," the old man said, stepping from behind the desk and extending an unwavering hand. "I'm pleased to meet you at last."

I gave him a questioning look as he took my hand. The grip of his spindly old fingers was surprisingly strong.

"Oh, I read the articles you wrote for the *Journal of the Southwest* on O'odham hunting legends," Power said. "Very well done. Very thorough."

"You must read a lot," I said.

"Oh, yes," he said, crossing back behind his desk and dropping down into the chair. "I read everything."

With a nod he indicated a chair, and I eased down into it. It was leather without too much padding—stiff and cold—and it rested slightly lower than I expected. So close to the front of the huge desk and down so low, it seemed intended to give its occupant the feeling of being a child suddenly thrust into a frightening position in the adult world. I wondered if the legs hadn't been sawed off. I slouched down, trying to make myself comfortable.

"You must have a lot of free time," I said.

He frowned.

"Do you know who I am?" he asked.

"I've read about you in the papers."

"Yes . . ." His gaze focused quietly on the desk before him as if he were considering my answer carefully. "And do you know why I invited you here?" he said finally.

"It wasn't much of an invitation," I said, looking around the room. In addition to the bookcases, there were marvelous canvases on every wall. A huge old globe, fully three feet across, rested in a stand at the far end of his desk. Power followed my gaze.

"Have you traveled much, Mr. Napoleon?"

"Here and there."

The old man smiled.

"I was in Paris in 1933," he said.

"The lost generation."

"More like a nephew of theirs. I was younger, barely in my twenties. I did run into Hemingway once, though, in a bar on Boulevard Montparnasse. Of course he was the Great Hemingway by then, The Writer, and I was just a schoolboy from Pasadena."

I shifted in my chair, feeling the cool hard leather firm against my back. The old man continued.

"Hemingway was at the end of the bar when I entered. It was raining, a sudden summer storm, and I hadn't finished shaking the water from my jacket when I noticed him. You must understand, I was a great admirer of the man. I had been fired from my job as assistant editor of the *Orange County Sun* when my father, upon making a surprise visit to the paper, discovered that I had walked away from my desk to hole up in a utility closet with a review copy of *A Farewell to Arms*.

"I'd carried the book with me to France, and when I saw Hemingway, I turned and walked quickly out of the bar. As soon as I was beyond sight of the front window, I broke into a run. I covered the seven blocks to my pension in what for me was record time. In my room I pulled the well-read copy of *A Farewell to Arms* from the shelf. Then I paused for a moment and considered the situation. On the shelf I had also a copy of *Father Saint, and Other Poems*, an early, almost unknown work Hemingway had privately printed and which even then was hard to find. I shoved the novel back, tucked *Father Saint* under my coat, and ran back to the bar.

"So there I sat. Sweating in the warm, crowded bar. The thin book clutched under my arm. I moved a few seats closer and waited for an opportunity to present itself. One of the men—boxing promoters from their looks—glanced my way, then scowled and ignored me. Hemingway himself was rapt in conversation with a slight young black man—no taller than myself, but wiry, with muscles in his shoulders and arms that slithered all over when he moved. I recognized him from the papers. Joe Jefferson, the lightweight champion. In Paris to defend his belt. The group went on ordering drinks, and Hemingway and the fighter continued their animated conversation. I nursed along a beer and finally as I signaled the barkeep for another, Hemingway turned my way.

" 'Well,' he said. 'You've been sitting there long enough, boy, and from the looks of you a second drink will put you on the floor. So tell us what you want.' He grinned, and the men in the group smiled, except for the fighter, who leaned back with a watchful look.

" 'I'd like an autograph,' I said, stepping forward.

" 'I'm sure Mr. Jefferson will be happy to give you an autograph, if you ask him politely,' Hemingway said.

"I was confounded. He was toying with me. The men around him smiled.

"I turned to the fighter and said that I meant no offense but that I was an admirer of good writing and a collector of books, not a fight fan. 'It's his signature I'd like,' I said, indicating Hemingway. The fighter shrugged, unimpressed. But clearly I'd made a mistake. Hemingway's face turned dark with anger. 'There'll be no autographs today,' he said. 'Not for one who doesn't know greatness when he sees it.'

" 'But—'

" 'No butts. Unless it's yours disappearing out the door.'

"I set my jaw. I couldn't believe I was to be denied. How soon might I get another opportunity such as this? A feeling I had hardly ever known washed over me. The autographed book suddenly became something I coveted. Something I could not bear to be without. I needed the book, and now was the moment to make it mine."

I shifted uncomfortably. I didn't know what the old man was getting at, and I was beginning to wonder if he did himself. I opened my mouth to speak, but Power continued before I could make a sound.

"The group had closed ranks. Hemingway returned to his conversation. I bulled through the two men nearest me and put one hand on the writer's shoulder. In the other I held the book. He turned and looked at me hard. I returned the gaze. Finally I pulled my hand away.

" 'Okay, boy,' Hemingway said, rising. 'You want your signature? I'll tell you how it will be. You take Joe's best shot, and I'll sign your book. Otherwise, you can take your hunt elsewhere—perhaps to the used book bins down on the Quais des Augustins. If you don't fall in the river.'

"I considered the proposal for a moment—only a moment, mind you—then I agreed. You see, Mr. Napoleon, I had to have that signature. I would stop at nothing.

"Hemingway urged the fighter to his feet. I faced him. The entourage formed a circle around us. Bets were exchanged. They were betting not on whether I would be knocked down, or even out, Mr.

Napoleon. They were laying odds on whether I would be killed.

" 'Okay,' Hemingway said. 'Go ahead, Joe.' The fighter pulled back, and I flinched, shutting my eyes tightly, concentrating merely on not fainting before the blow came. I felt the fist dig into my shoulder—a gentle tap by the fighter's reckoning, which nonetheless rocked me back on my heels. I opened my eyes and the fighter was smiling at me as one would at a plucky child. I smiled back.

" 'Well, boy, I guess you get your autograph,' Hemingway said. And as he stepped toward me his arm churned back and forward in a piston motion from the shoulder, his meaty fist driving into my belly just above the belt. I fell to the floor in a heap. The book popped out of my hand. Hemingway bent over and picked it up. Pulling a pen from his pocket, he signed it. He paused, staring at the title page for a moment.

" 'Been a while since I've seen one of these,' he said at last, scratching his jaw with the pen. Then he threw the book on the floor next to me. The promoters laughed, and bets were settled as they stepped over me and walked out of the place. And for a long time I lay there on the dirty floor of the bar trying to catch my breath, a pained smile on my face, the book clutched tightly to my ribs."

Power seemed to have finished. I didn't know what to say. It was a remarkable story. But what the hell did it mean?

"Interesting," I said. Power held up a hand for silence. He cleared his throat terribly, the rattle coming from deep within.

"That was sixty-two years ago. I still remember how it hurt when he hit me. That pain. But I also remember the satisfaction I felt. Because I knew I had won. Even at that moment, I knew I had chosen the right book. And I had acquired the signature. The volume I speak of is here."

He walked to the vast bookcase behind him and without hesitation pulled a thin book from an ocean of possibilities. Next to it on the shelf I could just make out the cover of a worn copy of *A Farewell to Arms*. Power thumbed gently through *Father Saint*, then set it carefully on the desk.

"It is one of a kind. Nearly as scarce as Poe's *Tamerlaine*. Very valuable. To the right collector, priceless.

"I'm eighty-nine years old, Mr. Napoleon. Hemingway . . . he's dead. I outlived him. I outlived them all. My doctor can find nothing wrong with me. I have buried four wives and innumerable lovers. I have beaten all of the actuarial tables. My doctor tells me the only thing wrong with me is something for which there is no cure. Age. He tells me I should quit seeing him. But still I go every six months. I tell him, as long as Medicare is picking up the tabs for our conversations, why should we stop? He doesn't argue. He has in his office a rare Apache Kachina, carved from a cottonwood root—rough and crude, primitive and quite exquisite—perhaps two hundred years old. Each time I visit, I offer to buy it from him. He can name his price. Someday he will give in and I will add it to my collection . . . but I see that you think all of this has nothing to do with you."

I tried to change my expression from growing boredom to open interest.

"Why don't we change the subject?" Power said. "Tell me about yourself and the recent events in your life. Tell me, Mr. Napoleon, about the body."

I stared at him for a moment.

"What's to tell?" I said finally.

"All," he replied.

"I had a body. It disappeared. Friend of mine named Ryder Joaquin. I feel responsible, although I don't know how I could have prevented it, and I'm going to try to find him, because his family needs to give him a proper burial. None of us are going to sleep very well until that's taken care of.

"Meanwhile, I've been knocked around like a weather balloon in a monsoon—at least partly by two guys who work for you—and the last I looked, my apartment was ready for disaster relief, the result of their handiwork as well."

"I apologize for Ben and Jerry," Power said.

I raised my eyebrows in disbelief.

"Ben and Jerry?"

"Yes," he said. "Those really are their names. They've been with me a long time—since long before the ice cream magnates were around. And they've always been a team. I'd hate to break them up."

"It'd be a shame."

"Although, I must admit, they really haven't been themselves since the Cherry Garcia became popular. They seem unhappy. I suppose it's difficult. People laugh. In any case, I'll talk to them about

their tactics. As for your home, I'm afraid a certain amount of un-
pleasantness is unavoidable. I asked you a question earlier, and you
have not answered it," he said.

I looked at him blankly, trying to recall. Finally it came.

"Why you invited me?"

He nodded.

I shrugged.

"It is really quite simple. I too have lost something. And I want
very badly to get it back."

Eleven

"Are you familiar, Mr. Napoleon, with the traditional O'odham method of recording history?"

"Calendar sticks?"

"Precisely."

"Sure."

Calendar sticks are the O'odham answer to the question of how you record history when you don't have a written language. Long before the white man taught them his letters, the O'odham came up with their own solution. They took the long, straight rib of a saguaro cactus and carved it into a smooth wooden pole the size of a hiking staff. Starting at one end of the stick, they carved nicks and gouges in the wood to represent significant moments in their history. Each village had its own calendar stick, and the keeper of the stick would memorize the stories that went with each mark, passing them down generation to generation. "Here is when the rains came for three weeks and the big river flooded," the keeper would say, pointing to a nick carved in the wood a hundred years before, "and here is where the Apaches attacked for many days and drove our people south. This is when an evil shaman was discovered in the village and put to death." Or, pointing to the oldest known mark, "this is the night the stars fell from the sky."

"You are aware," Power said, "that traditionally, each village had its own stick?"

"I'd heard that."

"Perhaps you have also heard that these artifacts occasionally materialize. That is to say, they're uncovered. I'm not talking about anything stolen, but rather legitimate discoveries—most often the stick is a forgotten relic from a now-vanished village, until it is dug up."

"I guess," I said.

"I recently acquired just such a stick, Mr. Napoleon. Or rather, I located one. Which I then purchased. It was to have been delivered to me, but I'm afraid I never received it. My intention was to donate the stick to the State Museum at the university. But now . . . who knows what might happen to it? You must realize that such an artifact would be quite valuable?"

I nodded.

"If it were found by an unscrupulous individual," the old man continued, "it might be sold—perhaps to a party that could afford to pay more than I. And wouldn't it be awful if it ended up in the warehouse of some Japanese corporate giant—just another objet d'art, purchased for its insurability and potential resale value?"

"Awful," I said. "But I still don't understand what it's got to do with me."

"Everything, Mr. Napoleon, it has everything to do with you. Because I am quite certain that when you locate the body of your friend—*if* you locate the body of your friend—you will also find my calendar stick."

Power had continued for a while—hinting at how much he was willing to pay for the stick if it were returned, but never coming right out and naming a price. He didn't say why he believed it would be with Ryder's body, or how it got there. When I questioned him on those points he was evasive. I got the feeling the whole thing was a game to him—something to occupy his time while he went on beating the actuarial tables. But it was clear he was serious about one thing. He wanted the missing calender stick.

I had thought about explaining to him that I didn't really believe such an object could belong to him in the first place. If a calendar stick—an authentic one from before the turn of the century—turned up, it would belong to the village it came from. If the village no longer existed, it would be up to the O'odham Nation to decide ownership. Probably it would stay with the tribe, maybe be displayed at tribal headquarters, or used in ceremonies. But the days when those pieces went directly to a wealthy collector, or the State Museum, were over. And despite his protestations, it was clear the old man really wanted the calendar stick for his personal collection. And I wasn't eager to help him add to that.

The money didn't really interest me. I didn't need anything, except peace of mind. And I wasn't going to find that in the foothills.

Still, I hadn't said anything. There was something about the man that was captivating, entrancing. The proverbial snake charmer. And that shifty, indefinable power had kept me from voicing my objections.

What was that? Fear? I didn't think so, but maybe . . .

The thin man was waiting for me outside Power's office, and he guided me back down the long hallways.

"Quite a collection," I said as we approached the front door.

He didn't bother replying.

The sun was so stingingly bright it made my eyes ache as I walked out of the cool dark foyer. Stepping into the heat was like walking into an oven. I crossed to the Jeep, blinking against the sun. Ben and Jerry were waiting inside, with the motor running, the windows rolled up, and the air-conditioning cranked.

I watched them through the windshield. Apparently they were arguing, or at least discussing something important. The short man was all red in the face, and he gesticulated wildly with his hands as he spoke. The sloppy one just shook his head quietly, patiently, side to side.

By the time I made it over to the Cherokee, he had the back door open. The short one stayed in the driver's seat.

"Please . . ." the sloppy one said to me, indicating the back seat.

"Are you Ben?" I asked. "Or Jerry?"

"Get in," the short man growled.

"Maybe you could just direct me to the nearest bus stop," I suggested.

"We'll take you," the short man said. "Just don't scuff up the upholstery."

"To be exact," the sloppy one said, "please keep your feet on the floor."

"So you're . . . ?" I said as I climbed in.

He shut the door in my face.

Twelve

They took me back to my place and dropped me off. As I walked in the front door, a surreal feeling washed over me. The idea that those two goons—however comical their names—had my address and felt they could kick my door in any time they wanted, went a long way toward subverting my reality. I'd worked long and hard to slip through the cracks—cultivating a life as near to the fringe as I could get without drying up and blowing away all together.

I didn't have credit cards, or a mortgage, or car payments. I had done my best over the past few years to live as near as I could to the ideal I remembered John D. McDonald espousing in the Travis McGee novels of my youth. No connections. No debts. Few real friends. Fewer enemies.

I hadn't owned a serious weapon since the old days. I gave all that up after the FBI raid. When I came back to the desert, the rage that once owned me had seeped away. And the old tools just seemed to lead to trouble. I had a couple of hunting rifles around for a while—but one day when rent was long overdue, I realized I was never going to hunt another living thing again, and I sold them.

I had a pistol, then, too—a .357—but I'd gotten rid of it a while back, when my neighbor, Bob, was attacked by one of society's depraved legions.

Apparently when this drooling psycho broke into Bob's place—and hid behind the bedroom door—he was counting on surprising an unsuspecting coed. What he got instead was a 200-pound, Brooklyn-raised, Sicilian-blooded ex-Marine. Bob surprised the wacko and fought him to the ground, breaking his own hand and the sicko's jaw in the process. This was a sexual deviant, with a long record of offenses, who put up a hell of a fight despite the fact that he wasn't wearing any pants at the time. As it turned out, he was also a college professor from a university up north, who apparently just rode the bus down to Tucson once in a while, when the urge took him. The judge let him walk on five hundred dollars bond. The professor caught up to Bob in the hall outside the courtroom. "It'll never go to trial," he whispered. "You'll never live that long."

When Bob told me about it a week later, I gave him the .357, saying "Maybe you ought to hold onto this for a while. I don't really need it anymore." Bob was still waiting for the case to go to trial.

But I was starting to wonder if I'd been right. Maybe it wouldn't be such a bad idea to arm myself—a little protection in case the ice cream boys decided to call again. I would have to think about it. Carrying a gun, even owning one, is a bigger decision than most people realize. And unfortunately the fringe groups are doing nothing to dispel that delusion.

But first things first. The place was still a mess and it was going to be a big job restoring it to its original state of disorder.

As I started straightening up, I noticed that the number of messages on the answering machine had grown in my absence. The display was blinking 4, over and over. You're letting things pile up, Napoleon, I scolded myself. But I chose to ignore it, sticking to the task at hand.

I spent a couple of hours picking things up and putting them away, righting the furniture, and shoving books back onto shelves.

Finally, when it was looking more or less livable, I sat down to make some phone calls.

If I was going to find Ryder's body, I needed to know more about how he'd been living in Los Angeles—and how he'd died.

I dialed the operator and found out that Los Angeles County had two area codes. I called directory assistance for both, but didn't find a listing for Sandy Asoza. There was an S. Asoza in West Hollywood, but when I tried it, a sleepy, effeminate voice told me that there was no Sandy there. *"S is for Siegfried,"* he said. I hung up.

I decided to try a different angle and I dug the piece of paper with the LAPD phone number out of my dirty jeans.

It rang and rang. Finally a voice barked, "Yeah?"

"Detective Furber?" I said.

"Not here."

"Well, is there any way I can get hold of him, or leave a message?"

"He was here earlier, don't know where he is now. I'll take a message if you can hold on a sec—"

"Sure," I said, but the phone had already clunked down at the other end.

There were some shuffling noises and finally the voice came back. "Furber, you said?"

"Yeah, I'm calling from Tucson about a—"

"Oh, shit, this one doesn't work either. Hold on another minute," and, clunk, the voice was gone.

"Can't ever find a goddamn pen that works around here," I heard in the background. More shuffling and the phone was picked up again.

"Okay, message for Furber. From?"

"Napoleon. Gray Napoleon."

"Napoleon . . . like the country?"

"Wha—yeah," I said. "Sure."

"Okay, Napoleon, regarding . . . ?"

"A homicide."

"Yeah, yeah, that's all we got. Which homicide?"

"Guy named Joaquin. Ryder Joaquin."

"Spell it?"

I did, and I left my number and said I hoped the detective would call me.

"Me, too," the voice said. "But don't waste your life waiting by the phone. Furber's usually here early mornings, if you don't hear from him, try then."

"Thanks," I said, but the line had already gone dead.

So that wasn't going anywhere fast. What I needed was someone who could do a little footwork for me.

I had a friend who, last I heard, was working for the *L.A. Times.*

I first met Mike Gould on a plane ride out of Saigon—a little more than a month after I escaped from the bamboo-roofed pit in the prison camp, and ran and walked for three days through the jungle to friendly country. I'd sat back against the steel wall of the transport plane, swallowed hard, and closed my eyes as we lifted off.

When I opened them again, we were in the air. And when I looked over at the guy next to me, he was smiling a weak smile and fumbling in his shirt pocket for a cigarette. His face was drawn and pale, sweat had broken out over his forehead.

"I think I know," he said, "exactly how you feel."

I smiled and reached over, pulling the pack from his shirt pocket. I took one out and lifted it to his mouth, filter first. He accepted with a nod.

Mike was missing his right arm. His left was still there, but it ended in a thick, gauze-wrapped stump, with only the thumb free—like wearing a thumbless boxing glove.

He nodded for me to take one for myself, and I did, then I shoved the pack back into his pocket.

"No smoking back there," someone growled, and Mike and I exchanged a glance, leaving the unlit cigarettes in our mouths. It was better than nothing.

We got to talking and it turned out he was from a little mining town in New Mexico called Mogollon.

I remembered driving through the place and over a high mountain pass on one of those summer trips when I was eleven or twelve.

"Like something from the movies," I said. "It looked like it was built for an Alan Ladd picture."

He nodded and smiled. "Yeah, that's home."

He asked what I was going to do when I got back to the world. I told him I just didn't know.

"Thing is," Mike said, "I always wanted to be a writer—hell, I guess I've always been one. I signed up because my old man volunteered the last time around. I was working for *Stars and Stripes*—I was going to be a reporter when I got home—if I got home." He held up his bandaged hand. "Shit, man, what do you make of that?"

I shook my head silently. I didn't know what to make of it.

"They can't even tell me whether or not my hand's going to work again," he said. "I guess it doesn't matter. Can't be a reporter with one hand." Later he told me he'd gotten the wounds in a bar. A woman rode past the door on a bicycle, and the next thing he knew a package the size of a brick was flying through the window, landing on the floor next to his table. The two guys across from him were killed. The one next to him had walked away with a small scratch on his temple.

There was more—we talked about home, and hunting and fishing, about hiking into the high mountains in New Mexico and Colorado.

Then the plane landed, and we went our separate ways, and that might have been it, if we hadn't bumped into each other a few years later.

It was at a public meeting in Flagstaff, sponsored by the Department of the Interior. I was there with a couple of friends to ask a few questions about clear-cut logging on National Forest Land. But the question and answer period was cut short that day—like on so many others—and my group didn't get to speak.

Mike was at the meeting for his own purposes—he was covering it for the local daily. As it turned out, missing arm and all, he had talked an editor into giving him a shot, and apparently he was coming along just fine. When we got together after the meeting, he said, "Hell, I don't know what I was worried about. I just had to learn to type twice as fast as the next guy."

He gave me his number and address, and whenever I made it that way, I stopped by and we talked.

We had a lot of arguments back then—he understood my position, but Mike said that by going at it so radically (by then, Foreman was pulling us together into a band of "eco-warriors") we were making it harder for the other side to change. "Just like the protesters during the war," he said. I didn't buy the argument—in either case—but we debated the issues good-naturedly, then got drunk and let them go.

I was living in Tucson by the time Mike moved on to the *L.A. Times*—his fifth paper in seven years, each a little bit larger than the one before.

He sent me a note with his new address. "I think I'll be here for a while," was all the note said.

I knew he'd covered the police beat at one point, and a few years back I'd been surprised when I walked into a bookstore and saw a mystery novel with his name on the cover. I bought it and read it.

The book was about drugs and murders and dirty streets, which if you live in L.A. just about says it all, I guess. I liked it, though, and thought about writing him a letter, or maybe giving him a call—just to catch up and congratulate him. But like so many things it just slipped away.

Now, I dialed directory assistance and got the number for the *Times*. Mike, I was told, still worked there—covering cops same as always, although now he was an assistant editor. I wondered exactly what that meant. Probably that they hadn't given him a raise when he deserved one. In any case, I got through to his desk, and after a couple of rings, his thick voice answered, and immediately put me on hold.

After a few minutes he came back on.

"You still there?" he asked.

"Yep. Stirred but not shaken."

"Well, jesus-god, Napoleon, how are you?"

"Fine, just fine," I said, and we worked our way through the pleasantries, catching up quickly. I told him I'd read his novel and liked it, and he said there were three of them out now, and if a few more readers would buy them, he could quit his job.

Finally he said, "So you didn't just call to congratulate me on my ascension into the literary heavens, did you?"

"No. I need some help—with something that's right up your alley."

I told him about Ryder, the disappearance of his body, and my need to find out more about his death—and how he'd been living.

"And the detective is?" Mike said.

"Furber."

"Oh, hell. Him. Well, I'll find out what I can. But I wouldn't wait for him to call back—or even expect much if you track him down."

"That bad?"

"Worse. Can you hold on for a second?"

"Sure."

He was back in a moment.

"I gotta go, Napoleon. I'll dig up what I can and get back to you."

"Thanks," I said, and gave him my number.

There was an awkward pause. Finally he spoke again.

"You spiking any trees?"

"Not this week," I said.

"I'll call you back."

After that, I tried to reach Maria—her machine picked up at home. At her office I got her assistant, Steve.

"Hold on Gray, let me check," he said when I asked if she was around.

When he came back, he said, "Uhm, she's on another line. Busy morning around here. Maybe you should try her later."

I thought I heard something strange in his tone.

"How much later?"

"Can't help you with that. Later."

"Sure," I said. "Thanks anyway."

"Absolutely," he said, and clicked off.

I sat for a while, looking at the phone, wondering what to do next. Finally I looked up the number for the Ajo substation of the Sheriff's department. Cavroni and his partner were out on patrol. I left my name and number.

I was growing restless. I grabbed my keys and headed out the door, checking first to make sure the porch light was out, then carefully twisting the dead bolt all the way.

It was past noon and nearing a hundred and ten degrees. The sun shone down from straight overhead with that same blank, pitiless gaze Yeats saw in the eyes of the Sphinx.

I walked toward where I'd parked the jeep, then changed direction. I had done enough driving the last couple of days. A walk would do me good.

As I trudged up the sidewalk, I felt the sweat breaking out. Soon I found my stride and I was moving smoothly, rhythmically through the dry, raw energy of the heat.

At first I headed toward the Congress, but the thought of running into the French girl changed my mind. I wasn't quite ready to see her yet.

Instead, I turned and headed toward the tall buildings and ended up at a place called The Grill. It is funky—with blues on the box, strange art on the wall, and one room done entirely in red velvet. The ambience straight out of a David Lynch movie. It also serves the best diner food you will ever eat, bordering on gourmet. And damn fine coffee.

I had three glasses of ice water, eggs and toast, and two cups of black coffee.

I paid, left a generous tip, and walked out into the bright, white heat of the day. I made my way three blocks north and passed through the underpass—the tracks empty, silent overhead—and then up to Fourth Avenue.

I walked up the Avenue, glancing in the shop windows. Finally I came to an old bungalow set apart from the other buildings. The small yard was filled with wildflowers. Senna and primrose and locoweed, rabbitbrush and sacred datura. A hummingbird hovered over the Arizona thistle, sucking nectar from that bristly sunflower.

I opened the wrought iron gate, and followed the twisting brick trail up to the porch. The sign on the dark-tinted window said Ted Sayer, Indian Arts.

A small bell overhead jingled as I opened the door. It was dark inside and the coolness hit me like a wave. I stood still for a moment, letting my eyes adjust.

The two front rooms of the building are the business end, and waist-high glass cases run the length of the walls. Ted specializes in Indian art from up north—Navajo, Hopi, Zuni—but he also carries some Tarahumara work, and pottery from Casas Grandes.

The floors were wooden—wide slats of good old oak, stained brown, here and there showing the black signs of ancient nicks and gouges.

"If you see anything you like, let me know." The voice floated quietly out of the far corner of the room. I turned toward her, squinted into the darkness. She was short and thick, with dark hair and dark skin, sitting in a chair behind the jewelry case, rubbing a silver ring with a soft cloth.

"All of it. But actually, I'm looking for Ted."

"He's out back," she said. Then added, "Do you want me to get him?"

"Sure."

She rose slowly and carefully slipped the piece of silver into a slot in the case—I could see clearly now it was Hopi, with the traditional water pattern—and then she slid the case shut, crossed the room, and disappeared through a doorway.

I worked my way along a row of cases while I waited. In one case

I found a small group of Zuni fetishes—pieces of polished rock carved into animal shapes. For the Zuni, the spirit of the animal resides within the fetish. A black bear with a piece of turquoise strapped to his back caught my eye. If I remembered right, the bear would be taken along by a hunter seeking a bighorn or other mountain sheep. Next to it was an owl on a leather thong, to be worn around the neck—not really a fetish, then, just a superb piece of Zuni carving.

"She says you like all of it," a voice said behind me. "Means you have good taste."

Despite the creaky wooden floors I hadn't heard him enter the room.

Ted is tall and thick. Appearing as he did now, in sloppy jeans and a half-unbuttoned workshirt, with his gray beard trimmed short and a red bandana over his head, he looked like an overgrown version of Willie Nelson.

The face was tanned dark from the sun and chiseled with thick, sharp lines. The nose was long and straight. The silver hair touched his shoulders in back. The blind eyes were hidden behind dark aviator sunglasses.

"You move pretty quiet for a big man," I said.

"Napoleon?" he asked. "That you? How the hell are you?"

"I am tolerably well, considering I've been here five minutes and you haven't offered me a cold beer."

"Well, you know where they are. Grab two and follow me out to the shop. Oh. Did you meet Lisa?"

"Not really."

"Lis," he said, "this is my old friend Gray Napoleon. Give him anything he wants—but mark it double first and don't turn your back on him!"

"Hi," I said.

She nodded quietly and smiled.

I followed Ted back down the hall. I jagged left at the kitchen and pulled two beers out of the fridge, then went out the back door, across the dirt yard to the workshop. It was a massive old structure with twenty-foot ceilings and a corrugated steel roof. The huge doors had been pushed open and the swamp cooler was running, but it was plenty hot in there.

Ted sat in a battered old wooden chair in the shade of a mesquite, just outside the door to the shop. I pulled a wooden crate over and sat on that, leaning back against the trunk of the tree.

"What happened to Nancy?" I asked.

"She left."

Nancy was Ted's third or fourth wife, I couldn't remember which—he goes through them fairly quickly, and fills the gaps between with a succession of temporary relationships. They all leave him in the end and I have never asked why. He is brilliant, well-read, an exacting and excellent craftsman. He can speak at length on a variety of subjects, providing specific and accurate information. He can drink more than I would ever like to and still stand and walk a tolerably straight line. Normally he is quiet and peaceful, but when his voice rises, he bellows like an aging Shakespearean actor. I imagine he's a pain in the ass to live with.

"Oh," I said. "Coming back?"

He leaned back in the chair, tilting his face up at the sky, letting the sunlight filter down on him through the small leaves of the mesquite.

"I can't say she is."

"Oh."

"Lisa is from Acoma. Just moved down from the pueblo. She says she'll help out at least through summer."

"That's good."

"Sure is."

We talked for a while, catching up on our lives. In addition to Nancy's leaving, he said he'd had to put his old labrador, Mel, to sleep a few weeks back—canine encephalitis, the vet had told him.

"It's not been a great summer so far," he said. "Maybe the monsoons will come and bring a change of luck."

I told him about Ryder, and how the body had disappeared. He shook his head.

"World's gone absolutely crazy," he said, "hasn't it?"

"Seems like," I said.

"You know, the older I get, every once in a while I'm glad I don't have to see it. I've gotten set up here now so I know the *feel* of things. You know I can tell the difference between alabaster and marble by touch?"

I snorted.

"Fact," he said. "I can tell almost all of them apart, polished or not. So I get someone to help me with the buying and selling, and I spend most of my time out here. When it's hot I feel the heat. When it's cold, I wear a coat. I like it."

"I hear a 'but' coming."

"I'm feeling old, Napoleon. Just lately I'm starting to feel old."

"Well," I said, taking a long drink off my bottle. "You are old," and we both laughed.

I finished my beer and said, "Another?"

"I'll get them."

I watched him walk inside, lithely, gracefully, never missing a beat. Anyone just looking in would not have known he was blind. A man could do a lot worse than this little world, I thought. In fact, most do.

He came back with the opened bottles, held one out, and I took it.

"So," he said, "you didn't know Nanc'd left, which means you can't have come here to comfort me. And if you were just coming to sit around and get drunk, you'd have waited until long after sundown, no?"

"Si. Actually I'm after information."

"Ahh, and I am the font. What is it?"

"Calendar sticks. Apparently, there might have been one in the box with Ryder. What I'm trying to figure out is how valuable it might be, and where it could have come from."

"We're talking about a fairly old stick here, I assume."

"I'd imagine. I know there are some O'odham who still make them and sell them to the tourists. But I think we're talking about an original."

"Well, the value then would be entirely relative."

"To what?"

"To the age of the stick, and to where it came from. Like anything, the price of artifacts, whether stolen—or misappropriated as the euphemists say—or not, depends on how much the buyer is willing to pay. If we're talking about a very old calendar stick, the kind you might see in a museum, say a hundred years or more—well, you're talking about a very elite class of buyer."

"How elite?"

"It wouldn't surprise me to see something like that go for tens of thousands of dollars. But that's just a starting figure."

"How high could it go?"

"Given the right stick, the right buyer, you might have an indeterminately valuable object."

"How do you mean."

"Well, say a stick comes from Comobabi, or one of the other villages close by Kitt Peak Observatory, and say on that stick is recorded the passing of Halley's Comet in 1835, and say you have a buyer who is a billionaire amateur astronomer."

"The connections give it value."

"Right, and exactly how much depends on what the connections are, and how much the buyer is willing to spend. What those connections would be, I don't really know. You'd have to talk to someone who knows more about the history and folklore than I do."

"Which brings me to my second question."

"And my third beer. How are you doing?"

I had hardly touched my second bottle.

"I'm good."

He went back inside, emerging with a bottle. When he'd gotten settled again, he said, "You were going to say?"

"That what I'm really interested in is if any museums or collections have recently been unburdened of anything along the lines of what we're talking about."

"A heist?"

"Exactly."

"Not lately. And not calendar sticks. There were two large art thefts in Europe last year—big museums, made all the papers. Here in the States, I've heard of one collection being burgled, oh six or seven months ago. But that was paintings, stolen from a Mormon millionaire in Salt Lake City."

"Not the kind of thing I'm looking for."

"No, and what's more, I don't think too many of the kind of stick you're talking about are actually around."

"What about the chances of one turning up somewhere? You know, up in the attic after Uncle Klaus dies—and the family always thought his tales of a great-grandfather who toured the Wild West were just good stories?"

"It's always possible. And probably the more likely explanation in this case. If an artifact like a calendar stick had turned up missing or stolen, public or private, I would have heard about it. It's a pretty small group, the people who deal in Indian art, and we're all connected on the Internet nowadays."

"I don't think this would have turned up on any computer bulletin boards."

"In which case a discreet phone call is still the best method. Word gets around, my friend, word gets around."

He finished his beer, and I let mine settle. Finally I got up to leave.

"By the way," I said. "What are you getting for the fetishes?"

"Which one?"

"Black bear."

"With turquoise?"

"That's the one."

"I think I remember it being thirty or thirty-five."

"Can't afford it. How about an owl on a leather string?"

"Fifteen."

"Sold."

"Have Lisa ring it up on the way out—and tell her I said you get the discount. You in trouble with Maria?"

"I don't know."

"Then you probably are. She'll love it."

We shook hands and he went back to his workshop.

I paid full price for the fetish, tucked it into my shirt pocket, and left, walking back down Fourth Avenue, the way I had come.

When I got back to my place, I tried calling Maria again. This time Steve didn't bother putting me on hold.

"Not available," he said.

I told him not to leave a message. I would try her later at home.

As soon as I put the phone back in the cradle it let out a shrill half-ring. I looked at it incredulously and waited. It rang again, and I picked it up and said hello.

"That you, Napoleon?" I recognized the soft, cranky voice immediately.

"Yeah, it's me."

"Well . . ." There was a long pause. Then, ". . . you know who this is?"

"Charlie?"

"Yeah. It's me all right. Hey, how's that foreign woman?" he asked. Then he laughed softly.

"Haven't seen her."

"Yeah," he said. "You hear anything yet?"

"No," I said. "You?"

"Well, maybe I did. But I don't know if it's important."

I let that one hang there. Which seemed to suit him fine, because after a moment he continued.

"Maybe I heard where Sandy Asoza is staying."

"That's probably important," I said.

"Only maybe you're not gonna like it."

"That's always a possibility."

"Yeah. Say, you want to come out here and meet me? I can tell you all about it. Thing is," he said, "Sandy left the country."

Thirteen

I put the key in the ignition and turned it clockwise. The motor turned over unhappily—uhna-uhna-uhna. I let off the key and pulled the choke knob out a little, tapped the gas a couple of times, and tried again. Uhna-uhna-uhna—BLAM!

The backfire was so loud I ducked reflexively, cringing from the noise. For the briefest moment, I had been truly and wholly convinced that I was going to die—that someone had planted a bomb on the frame of my vehicle and I was going to be ripped to shreds, just another fool who had started asking the wrong questions of the wrong people in the wrong state.

I sat back and took a deep breath as the motor gasped and coughed and shook with life, finally settling into a steady though ragged rhythm.

I gave myself a quick lecture on paranoia and nervous tension and the killer effects of stress. After a moment I felt fairly settled, and I pulled away from the curb, heading south and west through the city.

The incident helped me make one decision anyway. I suddenly realized that despite all my internal debate, I wasn't going to start carrying a gun. Not unless things got a lot worse than they were. If I was nervous now, walking around armed would just put me that much closer to the edge. And that was a place I didn't want to go.

When I got to Sells, the capital of the Tohono O'odham Nation, I found Charlie right where he said he would be—sitting in the shade outside of the town's one grocery store.

"Hey," Charlie said, and he slid in to the passenger seat.

He told me he had caught a ride into town that morning. He'd planned to pick up a few things for Ryder's mom, then catch a ride back at least as far as the crossroads that evening—from there either walk, or catch another ride if he was lucky.

At the store, he'd run into Flora Zepeda. Flora was from Quijotoa. She hadn't heard about Ryder dying, but she did know Sandy Asoza, and she said that after being gone for years, Sandy had returned home to Quijotoa a little while ago.

"How long?" I asked.

"A few days," was all Charlie could say.

In any case, it didn't really matter, because Sandy wasn't there anymore. Flora was sure of it, because she'd seen Sandy the day he left, hunched down in the passenger seat of his grandfather's pickup, pulling out onto the highway. Flora hadn't thought much of it at the time, but a couple of days later, two men came around looking for Sandy. Everyone agreed that they looked like cops, and nobody answered their questions, but Flora hadn't been convinced. They both wore slick clothes, and shiny boots, and they had glasses with very dark lenses.

Anyway, Flora found out the next day from Amelia Ortiz, who lived close to the Asozas, that Sandy had gone to stay with his grandparents.

Charlie said he'd thought about asking Flora to wait there with him, so I could hear it all for myself, but he'd decided against it. She wouldn't have been all that comfortable talking to me, and she never would have told me as much as she revealed to Charlie.

"Anyway," he said, "she had to go."

"Yeah," I said.

"So, what do you think?" He had a quiet, satisfied smile on his face.

"Pretty good."

"Yeah. But what do you think?"

"Of what?"

"Well," he said. "You want to go there?"

"Where?"

"Ce dagi Wahia."

It sounded familiar. I'd heard of the village before, but I couldn't remember where or when.

"Some people," Charlie said, "call it Poso Verde."

Poso Verde is a small village a few miles south of the line, in Sonora Mexico. I headed east on 86 to Three Points, then turned south. The sun was beating down hard, and the blacktop looked like a hot sticky mess. Charlie sat back in the passenger seat, eyes half closed, hot wind whipping at his silver hair.

I felt the beads of sweat form then dry over and over again on my face and arms as the wind wicked the moisture from my skin as quickly as it appeared.

The land was rough and dry and empty. There were no other cars on the road, and we were surrounded by cactus and rock, the distance measured only by the mountains.

We crossed the border at Sasabe without too much trouble and soon were following a dirt road south and west through the desert.

At Poso Verde we stopped in front of a small adobe building, and Charlie talked to some people he knew. When he came back to the jeep he was shaking his head.

"Gotta go back," he said.

"Back?"

He shrugged. "A little way."

I grunted and turned the jeep around. We bounced back up the dirt road, and after a few minutes Charlie pointed out a nearly invisible track leading away from the road.

"There," he said.

I turned off and followed the trail toward a low, rocky hill.

After a few minutes we came to the Asoza's ki. It was an adobe house with a good roof and a ramada on the west side. Black smoke rose in a thin column from somewhere behind the ki, climbing up into the cloudless sky like an evil genie rising from his bottle.

I started to get out, but Charlie just sat back in the passenger seat.

I relaxed and waited. After a minute or two, an old couple appeared around the side of the building.

He was short and thick with long, muscular arms and meaty hands. His hair was mostly gray, and if I'd had to guess, I'd have said he was somewhere in his early sixties. He wore old jeans, a work shirt, and cowboy boots. She was smaller, wearing a simple, patterned dress. Her hair was covered by a blue scarf.

At the front of the building, the man stopped and stared at us for a few seconds. Then he made his way slowly over to Charlie's side of the vehicle.

They conversed in O'odham for a long time, their voices soft and breathy, the words dry and quiet, as if spoken through wool-lined throats. Midway through the conversation I heard Charlie say my name, and I looked over. The old man glanced at me, then stared off into the distance. I nodded and smiled. His chin dropped ever so slightly in what might have been a nod.

They continued talking, and I began to wonder if we were in the right place. I heard Sandy's name mentioned a couple of times, but not much else that I understood.

Finally, Charlie put his hand out the window, and they touched fingers in a loose handshake.

The man looked at me for a moment, then shook his head.

"Good luck," he said, wishing me luck.

I nodded. "Thanks."

He turned and walked back to the ki. He said something to the old woman, and she looked our way, then disappeared around the side of the house, toward that column of smoke.

"Well?" I said.

"Well, Sandy ain't here."

"Yeah?"

"He was here for a while. Came home with them a few days ago. He stayed, but then he left last night."

"Did they say where he went?"

"Unh-uh. Didn't know. They said a truck came with two men in it, looking for Sandy. They weren't from around here. Course, they said they didn't know where he was. Then he left, without saying where he was going. They're kind of worried. We could tell them if we find him."

"Sure," I said. "But what now?"

"I don't know."

I started the Land Cruiser.

"We could go up there," he said, pointing toward the hill. "That's where Sandy stayed while he was here."

"Why'd he stay up there?"

"Don't know," he said with a shrug. "It is strange, though. Up there, that isn't a good place. That's Ho'ok ki."

I remembered the stories of Ho'ok, the wicked witch. Ho'ok's mother, a young basketmaker, had hidden the Sun's red kickball under her skirt, taunting the boy who was looking for it. Sun's kickball went up inside the girl, into her womb, and nine months later, Ho'ok was born.

Ho'ok had claws on her hands and feet, and she grew quickly. Soon she was driven from the village. For a while she lived in a cave, hunting like an animal.

"Ho'ok," Charlie said, "she was real bad. She would take babies from their homes in Poso Verde and rip them open—wrap their insides around the house so the parents couldn't get out. Then she took the rest of the baby up there."

"To Ho'ok ki," I said.

He nodded.

"Ho'ok took them babies up there and put them in a big grinding stone—pounded them up and ate them."

The People, I remembered, had finally killed the witch, with the help of I'itoi. It was one of those rare times when Elder Brother returned to this world after giving life to first man and first woman. The way I'd heard it, they invited Ho'ok to come to a dance, and I'itoi tricked her into smoking a special tobacco that made her sleepy. She fell into a deep sleep, and I'itoi carried her back to her cave. The People covered her with firewood, lit it, and blocked the entrance to the cave.

Ho'ok woke up in the blaze. She jumped up and down in pain— jumped so high her head struck the ceiling of the cave. Finally she hit it so hard, the rock split open. But before she could escape, I'itoi jumped up on top of the cave and stepped on the crack, sealing it.

"Up there," Charlie said. "You can still see I'itoi's footprint. Right on top of the cave where Ho'ok lived."

"And died," I said.

"Yeah," he nodded, "and died."

Charlie pointed the way, and we followed the jeep trail a short distance further. At the bottom of the hill, I stopped and cut off the engine.

"Sandy stayed up there," Charlie said. "On top of the hill. Above the cave, that's what they said."

I got out and stretched, but Charlie didn't make a move.

"You staying here?"

"Guess so," he said. "Never been up there before. Supposed to be a corral up there, or what's left of one. I don't know."

The hillside was covered with ocotillo, and their tentacular arms—some of them nearly thirty feet tall—bobbed in the breeze like giant false eyelashes.

I scrambled up among them, making my way toward the cave.

Up higher, the hillside was covered with the orange and black shards of shattered pottery. I stepped carefully among them. For some reason—I wasn't sure why—I wanted to avoid disturbing the already broken clay.

A few feet more, and I came to the cave. It was actually two caves, the bigger of which was split apart at the top, the blue sky visible beyond the few boulders that had been lodged in the fissure. In the other cave I found the shattered remains of a large grinding stone.

I crossed around the side of the hill and scrambled up to the summit.

The view was magnificent—wide open in every direction. The small houses of Poso Verde looked like they were an arm's reach away.

The ground was rocky but fairly level, and I could make out the ruins of a stone wall—the corral, I assumed.

I walked over and knelt down, examining the ground. It was scuffed, the grass trampled down. Someone had dug a small fire pit, a few sticks of half-burnt wood in it. All in all it looked like a fairly unremarkable campsite.

As I turned, something caught my eye. The ground up here was black and craggy—volcanic rock with patches of sage, a few ocotillo, and a couple of barrel cactus. But a few granite stones had been dragged up from somewhere else, and I noticed that some of them had been separated from the others, and set in a straight line, leading to the fissure above the cave.

There were five of them, and I hiked up to where they had been laid out, running roughly north to south, about two feet apart. As I got close I saw the markings, and realized that these five had been chosen because they were flat and about the same size—roughly eight inches long and six inches wide. Each was covered with the same drawing, the black lines rubbed onto the stones with charcoal from the fire:

I walked around them to the crack in the ground, looked down into the cave. No more impressive from up here than from down below. But standing back, I was pretty sure I could make out I'itoi's footprint.

I scrambled back down to the jeep. Charlie was waiting patiently, eyes closed. The sun had dropped down below the line of the bikini top, and it was beating on the side of his face, but it didn't seem to be bothering him.

I climbed in and started the Land Cruiser, turned it around.

We drove slowly back down the trail, past the Asoza's ki, to the road. I turned left, and soon we were rocketing along toward the border, a thick rooster tail of dust trailing behind us.

After we crossed the border I headed north, toward Three Points. A few miles up the road, Charlie pointed out a jeep trail that cut off to the west, I followed it around the southern end of Baboquivari, and in a while we were pulling up at the Joaquins' ki.

Theresa Joaquin came out to greet us, and I told her about the events of the day, as Charlie pulled his small bag of groceries from the Land Cruiser.

"It's a start," she said when I was done, and she gave Charlie a look as if to say, "See?"

I told her I would keep trying, and reminded them both to call me if they heard anything more. Then I nodded and drove north, toward Kitt Peak, and the long road home.

Fourteen

*A pointy-toed boot nudges me in the ribs and I open
my eyes. I am in the desert outside of Sells. It is night
and I am drunk—drunker than I should be, too drunk
to stand, maybe even to talk.*

*"Hey!" The voice comes with the sharp boot. I look
up at the dark shapes of two bronc riders silhouetted
against the firelight. Their faces are hidden in the
shadows of wide-brimmed hats, but I sense a
hardness in the glint of their eyes.*

*"Hey," the one says again. "Me and my friend here,
we're thinking about having a party."*

It is not an invitation.

"Scalping party," the other one adds.

The rodeo is over. I do not belong here.

*"Yeah," the first one says, "you got nice long hair." It
is not a compliment. I feel my guts tighten.*

A third form appears out of the darkness behind them.

"No, he's okay," Ryder says. "He's with me."

I blink dumbly.

*After a few minutes of rodeo talk—bulldogging,
throwing a loop, dallying on—the bronc riders leave.
Ryder slides down in the dirt next to me. He folds his
legs and sits quietly. I pass out again. When I wake
up, many hours later, with the sun rising over the
mountains, he is still there, waiting.*

I headed east toward Tucson on what was becoming my nightly run.
The gas station across from Nacho's was still open, and I pulled in.
Inside, I grabbed a couple of packages of chocolate donuts—

plastic packed poison—and a large cup of bitter coffee. I paid with a twenty, telling the cashier I would put what was left in the tank, and I walked back outside.

Across the highway, the parking lot of the bar was full—trucks and motorcycles and a few cars. I pumped my gas with my back to the place.

Then I got back on the road and headed for Tucson.

There wasn't much traffic going into town now; all of it was going the other direction. Still, I was almost to Kinney Road before I noticed the headlights. The twin beams didn't make an impression until they were very close—right on my bumper.

I adjusted the mirror so they weren't glaring directly into my eyes, and at the same time I eased off the gas pedal ever so slowly. This is my way of dealing with tailgaters and, in general, any other driver I find obnoxious: I slow down, decelerating gradually until they get bored and pass me. The trick is to let up on the gas so slowly that the clown behind you doesn't realize it's happening. If you drop back suddenly, it may be taken as an act of aggression. And then you'll have one more complication in your life. It's an easy choice if, like me, you're never in that much of a hurry to get where you're going next.

I was surprised when one light broke away from the other and pulled up beside me. It was then I noticed the third light racing to catch up from behind, and the fourth, and the fifth.

I looked over, and saw the gray beard whipping in the wind, the ratty T-shirt, the wrecking-ball stomach. He grinned. My guts tightened.

The second one had moved into place behind my left wheel.

Kinney Road was coming up fast—a convenience store on the corner, then the empty stretch down to the south end of the city. I could stop and make my stand—but as I glanced back in the rearview, I realized the bikers were out in force tonight, and while they had chosen not to beat me to death last time, things might be different this go-round.

When I thought about it, it didn't really make sense that they were coming after me at all. I had lost. They had won. I was the one who had woken up in the parking lot with my ribs tenderized.

Maybe they saw me as game—like rabbit or quail—in season year-round.

Whatever the case, when I looked over, the big man was reaching back behind him, pulling a very large, very ugly revolver from a holster there.

My heart rate jumped up, and the blood shot into my brain. I gripped the wheel tightly and leaned forward.

I was almost to the intersection now. Time to make a decision.

I looked over again, and the man was lifting the pistol, pointing it at my head.

I jerked the steering wheel. Tires screamed. The Land Cruiser's big, boxy body leaned hard against the suspension.

The biker skidded and dropped, and I saw the glint of sparks and chrome in the sideview, then I was crashing through the foliage on the shoulder of the road.

I gripped the wheel hard, fighting left and easing back onto the road. I looked in the rearview. I'd overshot the blacktop and cut a wide swath in the sage and creosote on the side of the road.

The second biker hadn't even tried to make the turn. I saw the bright red glint of his brake lights, then the swoop of his headlight as he cut across the median and doubled back.

The big one had apparently slid into the ditch, because I couldn't see any sign of him in the darkness.

I stomped hard on the gas, gunning the motor, the Land Cruiser shaking and rattling under me, protesting angrily as I pushed it to its top speed—somewhere around seventy-five miles per hour.

I spotted the lights in the rearview again as I neared the monument—white pinpoints swimming in crazy patterns behind me.

The sign said, You Are Entering Saguaro National Monument, A Natural and Wildlife Preserve, All Within Is Protected. Well, let's hope so, I thought, as I skittered around a sharp curve, heading into the darkness of the saguaro forest.

The road through the monument is a dizzying series of dips and turns—two narrow lanes that appear to have been painted over the uneven face of the desert as a careless afterthought.

The monument itself snakes along the backside of the Tucson Mountains. A thick patch of desert, with few roads and no homes.

I clung to the steering wheel, alternately working the gas and the brake, shuddering through the turns, trying not to lose too much speed, playing a precarious game with the Land Cruiser's high center of gravity.

In a minute I saw headlights swinging over the desert in my rearview mirror—closer now—like large flashlights waving back and forth, up and down, as the motorcycles started into the dips and turns.

I gunned through the last hard curve, feeling the back tires of the big old four-wheel drive slip across a gravel strewn section of the blacktop. For a moment I thought I was going to lose it. The back end fishtailed around, the tires slipping wildly, and I was certain the big old beast of a jeep was going to fade just a little too far, then catch and roll. I let up on the gas, fighting the steering wheel, my foot hovering over the brake.

Then I felt the momentum shift as the road straightened out. I eased out of the turn and stomped down on the gas. The Land Cruiser screeched furiously, accelerating.

I glanced in the mirror. They were coming fast. The hopped-up Harleys were not only quicker, faster, they also handled better through the corners.

Now I was on a straightaway, the quiet, burned-out shadows of Old Tucson flashing by on my right.

I looked again, and the first of the bikes was coming through that final corner. I heard the cranked up whine of the motor as its rider gunned out of the curve.

Ahead was the junction to Gates Pass Road. Time to make another decision. If I turned right and headed toward the hills, I wouldn't make it far before they caught me.

The road up to Gates Pass is a twisting, narrow strip of pavement cut into the rock at a steep angle. I'd have to drop the Land Cruiser down into second, and maybe even first gear to make the climb.

If I beat the bikers to the bottom of the hill—a big "if" as things stood now—their powerful, torquey engines would enable them to catch me quickly on the climb. I would be one big fish in a slow-moving barrel.

But what were my options?

I looked in the mirror again. Now more of them had broken out of the curve and were accelerating after me.

I felt panic begin to creep up inside, clutching my throat in its tight grip.

Think, damnit, think.

Then it came to me, and I knew what to do, if I could only make it that far.

I shot past the junction. The spindly branches of palo verde and mesquite clawed at my headlights like trees in a child's nightmare. Beyond, was the darkness of the desert, the tall, haunting silhouettes of the saguaros.

I careened through another wide curve. I was concentrating on the road now, juicing the Land Cruiser for everything it had.

Suddenly my shoulders were illuminated brightly. I risked a glance in the rearview and caught sight of two headlights, very close, directly behind me—staying with me now as I pulled through another tight corner.

Then the road dropped out from under me and I was floating.

Then the Land Cruiser bottomed out. The last big dip. It had been enough to slow the bikes a little, and as I pulled up on the far side, I'd gained a few feet of space.

The Land Cruiser was rattling like a clapboard shack. The engine screamed. I glanced at the speedometer: *90*. Far beyond its supposed limits.

I heard the chopping roar, saw the swing of the headlight, as one of the bikes shot ahead of the others, pulling into the lane next to me.

I looked over and saw the gun already raised in the left hand, the arm buffeted by the wind.

I ducked, heard the slap, saw the shattered pattern, and then I was braking hard.

I gripped the wheel, fighting the skid. The shooter flew by me, but the others were right up on my tail. Then I let up on the brake pedal, yanked the wheel right, and once more I was skidding onto a smaller road.

This one led past the monument visitor's center—closed and dark, the parking lot empty.

The bikes were a jumble of chrome-reflected confusion behind me.

I jerked the Land Cruiser into second gear, gunned the gas, and shot up the one-lane road.

I flicked off my headlights, and leaned forward over the steering wheel, straining to catch sight of the thin ribbon of blacktop as I barreled through a couple of hairpin turns.

This was the tricky part. There wasn't enough light to see clearly, and if I missed the turnoff, or they came after me quickly enough, it would all be over.

Once, I skittered off the road, kicking up dust and skidding a little sideways before I found the pavement again.

The bikers would be on me in a minute, but the service road was just ahead. It was a small, unmarked stretch leading back to the business side of the visitor's center, its entrance hidden between two palo verdes. Thankfully, it was paved. The irony of that thought ran through my mind—me being thankful for a paved road, that was a kick. But then I was there, and turning, looping back in the direction I had come, switching off the ignition, and floating silently to a brakeless stop as the first of the bikers came roaring around the corner.

I wouldn't have long, and I knew it.

The main road ended only a few hundred yards farther along— it didn't end really, but the pavement did. And it wouldn't take them long, once they got that far, to realize that there wasn't any dust kicked up on the dirt road ahead of them. And that, combined with a lack of head and taillights, would indicate that I was no longer in front of them. It wouldn't take them long, but it should give me all the time I needed.

As the group roared by just a few feet away, their lights flickering past on the other side of the palo verdes, I hopped out and ran around the front.

In a few seconds I had the hubs locked for four-wheel drive, and then I was back behind the wheel, throwing it in reverse, spinning into a bootlegger's turn, heading up the road after them.

My timing was perfect. I negotiated the last few turns by feel, my headlights still off. I reached the place where the blacktop turned to dirt a few moments after they did.

They had stopped already, less than a hundred yards along the dirt road, the big man at the lead, his hand held up to the others.

Over the rumble of their engines, and their yells as they tried to communicate, I don't think they heard me until I was almost on them.

At the last second, I flicked my lights on, illuminating the surprised faces in front of me.

Then there was the scramble to move—a couple of the bikers abandoning their bikes at the last second, diving for the scrub brush.

They scattered like bowling pins. All but the big man. He was in the middle of things and had nowhere to go. He hopped off his bike—already scraped and dented from the first wipeout a few minutes before—and scrambled for the side of the road. My front bumper caught the Harley by the back fender and sent it spinning like a child's toy.

Then I was beyond them and pounding through the first turn in the dirt road.

I knew they wouldn't follow. Or if they did, it wouldn't matter. Here on the dirt was the one place I could go faster than they could.

On their motorcycles, they would have to crawl along on the loose dirt road. With the four-wheel drive engaged, the Land Cruiser had far superior traction.

I jounced down a hill and slid through another corner, then slowed to a comfortable speed, following the dirt road through the darkness.

Fifteen

The lights of Tucson lay before me.

I stayed on the dirt roads all the way through the monument, cutting far back into the saguaro forest on unused jeep trails.

The bullet had gone through my windshield to the right of the rearview mirror and a spiderweb of cracks ran all through it.

I wove my way up through the hills and down to the Interstate. It was a straight shot downtown and I putted along at fifty miles an hour, hoping I wouldn't get pulled over for the windshield. I didn't and soon I was exiting the freeway, disappearing into the barrio.

I was tired through to the marrow. My ribs and arms and shoulders ached. I had dust in my hair and eyelashes, and dirty grime down my collar and back.

I found a place to park and limped to my door. Once more I turned the key with some trepidation.

But the room was empty, and clean, the swamp cooler blowing a refreshing, soft smell.

I looked at the clock. It was ten-thirty. Later than I'd expected.

I dialed Maria's number. Her machine picked up after one ring, and I waited for the beep, then told her I was home, and explained that I hadn't called her sooner because I hadn't been near a phone. I also said I would be going to sleep in a few minutes, but she could call if she wanted.

Then I called for a pizza. None of that red, white, and blue, cardboard-crusted pie for me, though. I phoned the Upper Crust, dialing the number from memory. The owner, Charlie, is a transplanted

New York Italian and the nicest guy you'd ever want to meet—though I wouldn't want to owe him money. He is big, and tough, with the wry sense of humor and the dark eyes of a man who has seen more than his share of hard endings. His pizza, cooked up in a tight little storefront just off Campbell Avenue, is perfection.

I turned on the shower, running the water hot, and watched the thick stream of brown muck sucked down the drain as I washed off the dirt. Not for the first time I questioned the sanity of driving around the desert in an open jeep. It was uncomfortable, hot, and dirty. But for a man in my position—no position at all—it was the only way to go. Not necessarily sane then, but simply the only real option.

After showering I put on a pair of shorts and a T-shirt.

I put a CD in the box. The pizza came, and with the familiar tones of Bach's Fourth Brandenburg Concerto filling the room—and my mind—I sat back on the bed and ate like a wolf.

After a while I slowed down. Then stopped altogether. I put the scraps in the fridge, checked the door to make sure I'd locked it. Turned out the lights, and climbed under the covers. As a second thought I got up and padded across the room, found the rail spike, and jammed it between door and frame.

Then I lay down and stared at the darkened ceiling. My body was tired, but my mind was wide awake, and I went back over the last couple of days in my head, trying to put things together, attempting to make some sense out of what had happened.

There were plenty of little connections, but an overall pattern didn't seem apparent.

Obviously someone, or some group, had stolen Ryder's body. The question was, why? The obvious answer was the one provided by Power—a valuable calendar stick had been in the box with Ryder. Whoever took the body was after the artifact.

But that raised a whole batch of new questions. Why had the stick been placed in the box? Why didn't Power have his goons get it before I picked up the body? Was it stolen? Probably. From where?

There were other questions. Where was Sandy Asoza? From what Charlie had found out, and the evidence I'd seen above Ho'ok ki, it looked like he had been running—or at least hiding out. Running from what? Why?

What about the French girl? I hadn't really bought her story—it just didn't sound right. It occurred to me that I should have asked Mike to check into her background, too. I decided I would call him tomorrow afternoon if I hadn't heard from him by then.

That left the thugs on the motorcycles. It stretched the imagination to think that they might be connected to all of this. I was pretty sure I had just been in the wrong place at the wrong time—the only guy at the bar without any friends and with an inflammatory bumper sticker on his vehicle. To them, I was the human equivalent of a scratching post. So far, though, I'd done all the scratching—if you ignored my aching ribs, which I couldn't, and my windshield, which, I reminded myself, I would have to get fixed right away.

I had one last thought as I drifted off to sleep. What was the meaning of the markings at Ho'ok ki?

Sixteen

I was groggy, my mind still coated with the thick shroud of fatigue. Something had woken me.

The phone rang again and I rolled out of bed, fighting through the sheets, padding across the room in the dark. Another ring. I found the phone, fumbled, dropped it on the floor, bent down and found the base, followed the twisting cord to the receiver.

"Hello." It came out a croak.

Silence.

I cleared my throat.

"Hello," I repeated.

Nothing.

I took the phone away from my head, checking to make sure I had the right end to my ear. No problem there. I put it to my cheek again and tried one more time.

"Okay," I said. "Anyone there?" No voice, but a noise came floating through in the background—a long, high howl, growing louder, then dropping off. I pressed the phone tight against my ear, listening for a second. There it was again. Unmistakable. A siren.

I listened a moment longer, hearing the wail grow slowly, steadily louder. I was just about to hang up when I heard the other noise faint, almost drowned by the siren, but suddenly there, and identifiable— breathing.

"Anyone there?" I said.

"Monsieur," she spoke so softly I almost missed it, coming as it did at the height of one of the siren swells.

"Yes, umh—" I searched my mind for her name, found it. "Caroline, is that you?"

Long pause. Then again, the voice so soft, hardly louder than her breathing.

"Oui."

"Are you okay?"

Quietly, "non."

Then she coughed—a deep, wet gag that hissed at the end.

"Where are you? What's wrong?"

"Please," she said. Then she coughed again. For a moment the line was silent, except for the sirens in the background. She gasped, and breathed again.

"Where are you?" I asked again, hearing the tension rising in my voice. "Where? Just say where."

"Hotel."

"The Congress?"

A long pause, then "oui."

"Okay, listen, I'm coming there now. Do you hear the sirens—go to the sirens. If you can't make it to the sirens, hang up and dial 9-1-1. Do you understand? 9-1-1!"

Silence.

"Caroline?"

Nothing.

I found the clothes I'd been wearing earlier, dragged them on, slipped into my shoes and ran for the door.

I smelled it as soon as I stepped outside. Faint, but pungent, and unmistakable. Smoke. And the sirens. Walking quickly to the Land Cruiser, I could hear them. They were very close.

I drove up to Fourth Avenue and turned left, watching the orange glow growing above the rooftops.

Seventeen

In January 1934, Public Enemy Number One came to town. When John Dillinger and his gang showed up, Tucson was just a sleepy little dust bowl—a few trailer courts, a beautiful old Spanish mission, the bank building, and the Congress Hotel. They checked into the Congress, thinking it looked like the perfect place to hide out. And for a while, it was.

Then early in the morning—or late the night before, depending on which way you're coming from—the hotel caught fire. An oil furnace in the basement went up, and the flames ripped through the elevator shaft. Soon the building was consumed in flames.

A few weeks later, one of the firemen noticed something unusual as he was flipping through the pages of a true crime magazine. Among the photos of the nation's most wanted fugitives was one of the hotel guests he'd helped rescue. Dillinger and his gang were tracked down and captured that day and extradited to Illinois.

The cops were already blocking off the street. I pulled into the parking lot at the end of the block and walked toward the hotel.

Two big engines were there already, the men scrambling to unroll and hook up their hoses.

Flashes of red and yellow and blue reflected in the blackened plate glass windows.

A huge crowd of club-goers—black tights and leather, white lipstick and dark eyeshadow—stood in the street, watching the show.

The cops were trying to establish a line and move the crowd back. I wondered vaguely what time it was, and realized it must be before one A.M., or the bar would have been closed.

The fire was out of control—the lobby and most of the second floor were engulfed in flames—and it was spreading, out and up. Thick black smoke poured through open windows on the second floor.

A few people were wandering around in pajamas and robes, their eyes vacant and dreamy.

One man was screaming at a woman in what sounded like German. "Mein pass! Mein pass!" he said over and over, pointing at the hotel.

I wondered if they had gotten everybody out. Apparently the rescue workers were thinking the same thing, because already they were running two ladders up against the west wall of the building, leaning them carefully against the windows of rooms the fire hadn't yet reached.

I walked quickly in that direction, looking through the crowd for the French girl. Too many people. I brushed past a girl with frizzy hair in a short black dress and a frilly white apron. She looked at me with excited eyes and smiled. I grimaced.

As I worked my way toward the back end of a fire truck, a cop grabbed me by the shoulder.

"Back!" he yelled.

I started to say something, but he held up a black-gloved hand and pointed. "Back!"

I gazed past him, getting a good look at the deserted west end of the building, then shuffled back into the crowd.

I circled around behind the crowd—the milling minions of morbidity, Agnew might have called them, if he were still alive, and if William Safire were still writing his speeches.

More fire trucks were arriving now, and the police began pushing the crowd farther back.

I made my way to the east end of the building, searching the profiles silhouetted against the bright orange flames of the fire.

The restaurant was going now, and the small bar at one end of the club called the Tap Room.

The gabled roof of the place was catching, the smoke drifting up through the huge red neon Congress Hotel sign held up there by steel scaffolding.

I ran into the same resistance at the other end. I could see that the cops had shut down all of the streets now, and the underpass. The east end of the building was empty except for the fire crew.

I backed off and began searching the crowd in earnest, asking a few sober-looking individuals if they had seen her, giving a brief description.

One boy with long brown hair, wearing a tall, black, medicine man hat thought he might have been talking to her earlier. "But, hey," he said, putting his hands up in the air, "I didn't know she was with someone." I shook my head, walking away.

She had sounded frightened, hurt. The real question was, where had she called from? She'd said the hotel. But where? The lobby? The public phones in the lobby were all in a row against one wall—old-fashioned wooden booths, the kind with a small seat and a light that comes on when you close the door. Even with the door of the booth open, it was unlikely I'd have heard the fire trucks above the noise coming from the club.

Where else? Her room? Possibly. If the window had been open, I might have heard the sirens. I looked up at the building. I could easily count to her room. The window was closed, the curtains drawn. The flames were just taking that end of the building, and the firemen were spraying it hard with their hoses. The room was filled with the orange glow of the fire.

I didn't really think she'd been up there, but as long as there was a chance . . .

I shoved my way up to the front of the crowd, found a cop and told him as briefly as possible about her phone call. I pointed up to her room.

"Second one from the corner," I said. "I don't know if she's in there or not."

He nodded, and got on his hand radio, explaining the situation to some faceless organizer.

I faded back into the crowd. Now what?

The fire crews were backing off, surrendering to the fire. One man crawled on the hook and ladder to the French girl's room, but he couldn't get close enough, the heat too intense, and he backed away.

The brick building, short and wide, had become a giant chimney, with huge licks of flame shooting forty or fifty feet into the air above it.

As I watched, the old sign sparked and flashed. One fluorescent light bar exploded. Then, with a crackling of electricity, it crumpled and fell in on the burning roof. Some of the kids in the crowd whistled and clapped, a few cheered.

I looked around. What if she hadn't actually called from the hotel, but close to it?

At my back was the train depot. Was there a pay phone there? Must be. I crossed the street and walked the length of the building. The office was closed, the lobby dark. Apparently the last train had come and gone for the night.

I hoofed around the far end and followed the tracks along the back of the building.

The rear door of the office opened onto a cement platform, and I could see the blue and white glow of a pay phone at the far end. As I drew nearer, I saw the handpiece of the pay phone. It was dangling at the end of the spiraled metal cord, pointing stoically at the shiny black puddle on the cement below.

There was a lot of blood. And a thin track leading down the steps on the far side of the platform.

My heart pounded hard and my breath quickened. I backed into the shadows and looked around.

That thing you see on TV where people just run up to the scene of a crime? That's bullshit. At least it is if you have any idea what you're looking at.

The first thing you think when you see a body or a big puddle of blood is, where's the person who did that? Behind me?

My eyes were already adjusted to the dim light and I looked all around the tracks, avoiding the empty, lighted platform.

Then I walked slowly, carefully around the platform to the far side. The trail ran down the steps, and at the bottom there was another big pool. Then it went on.

I found her near the east end of the building, lying on her stomach in the gravel, one hand against the wall.

Very gently I rolled her over.

I gagged.

She was so wet—like a thick coat of black paint had been splashed on her chest and throat. Her breath was a thin, faint, rattle.

The breathing hitched, then started. Hitched, then started. "Hold on," I said.

I felt her hand on my shoulder.

"They're just around the other side," I said.

Her grip tightened. She said something. No more than a whisper.

"Just keep breathing," I said, and began to stand up. She spoke again, the words a hiss.

I leaned in close.

"They found me," she said.

"It'll be okay," peeling her hand away.

"I ran . . ."

"Just hold on," I said.

Her eyes opened, and she stared up at the night sky. Her voice grew louder for a moment.

"Napoleon," she said, and then she said something in French that I didn't understand.

Then I was up and running, sprinting around the building and across the street, breaking through the crowd, and grabbing the first rescue worker I found—a paramedic who was standing near the end of a fire truck with a bottle of oxygen in one hand and a black box at his feet.

But even as he called for more assistance, and, along with a couple of cops, we hustled back over there, I knew somewhere deep inside that it wasn't going to make a difference. I'd gotten there far too late.

Eighteen

The phone rang four times, stopped.

Then the voice: "I can't take your call right now, please leave a message at the tone."

Beep.

Click.

"Let me try one more time."

"One more. The same number?"

"Yes."

The thick finger pressed the redial button.

Three long rings, then half of a fourth, and the line was picked up. Silence.

Finally, "Do you know what time it is?"

"Maria," I said, "it's Gray."

"Is that your answer?"

I heard the rustle of material and knew she was pulling the phone from her ear, getting ready to hang up.

"Wait! Maria—"

"What?"

"I need help."

"You certainly do."

I could understand her being put out that I'd woken her, but I was sure she could hear the seriousness in my voice. Why was she so cold?

"Maria, are you hearing me? I need you."

"Well, why didn't you think about that before you went running around with your little chippy?"

Chippy?

"I don't know what you're talking a—"

"You don't? Where were you last night? The night before?"

"I was home last night. I tried to call—"

"At ten-thirty-seven."

"The night before—I told you, it's a long story, but I was out on the rez."

"Then how is it that a friend of mine saw you checking into a room at the Congress with a . . . a . . ."

So that's what she was angry about. Tucson's a small town, people talk . . .

"Maria, I just gave her a ride. I dropped her off, that's all. Jesus, it doesn't even matter now."

"Why not?"

"She's dead."

I talked to her for a few more minutes, explaining where I was and what had happened, then I handed the phone to the detective.

"She wants to talk to you," I said.

He took the phone.

"Miss Kazhe, this is Tim Miller."

Pause.

"No, no charges. Yeah, material witness."

Pause.

"No, nothing like that. He's agreed to cooperate and we—"

Long pause.

"Fine. We'll see you shortly."

We sat in the small, dingy room, detective Miller and his partner, Garcia, on one side of the table, Maria and I on the other.

"What we're trying to establish," Miller was saying, "is the facts."

"And we're trying to help," Maria said. "But asking how well he knew the woman, after he has told you repeatedly that he only met her yesterday, is getting us nowhere."

Miller looked at me, his face a mask of polite inquiry.

"Did you sleep with her?" he asked.

"No, I—"

"Don't answer that," Maria said. "Why do you ask, detective?"

"He's already answered," Miller said. "For the record. Like I told you, I'm just trying to establish—"

"Have you found any signs of sexual assault?" Maria asked.

"Now wait a minute," I said.

"It's an ongoing investigation," Miller said. "But I guess it doesn't matter if you know—" he looked to Garcia for confirmation, and the other detective nodded"—there was no preliminary sign of assault, or any sexual activity at all. Of course, we'll have to wait for the autopsy to be certain . . ."

Maria nodded, and her shoulders relaxed so slightly I was sure the other two couldn't have seen it.

"I told you," I said.

"Gray," she said, "this is important. Shut up."

I did.

"Well, then," she said, "I think my client has told you everything."

And as far as she knew, I had. I'd told them how and where I met the French girl, and what I was doing out on the rez in the first place.

They had seemed a little doubtful when I first told them about what happened at Why, but the idea seemed to grow on them.

"I can check your story with the sheriff's department tomorrow," Miller said.

"Be my guest. And ask them if they're making any progress. I got the feeling it wasn't something they were going to devote a lot of time to."

I told them about the phone call, and how I had tried to find the French girl at the hotel. Fortunately, there were plenty of witnesses to my activities, including the cop I'd talked to—not the movements of a would-be killer.

I decided not to say anything about Power and the ice cream boys. I wasn't sure why—it just seemed best. Miller and Garcia would want to know why I hadn't reported the breaking and entering, the assault, the kidnapping. But I knew that as long as I didn't have anybody to back up my story, bringing Power into this would cause me nothing but trouble.

"Well," Maria said at last. "It looks like you two have a killer to catch. Maybe we should get out of your way."

"Looks like it," Miller said with a big yawn.

Maria slipped her purse onto her shoulder, then paused.

"Do you know how the fire started?" she asked.

Again Miller looked at Garcia. Garcia shrugged.

"As far as we know, it was accidental. Apparently there was some kind of party in the hotel lobby, and a food warmer was knocked over. Appears that started it, and it spread quickly. But we won't know for a couple of days—until after the investigators get in there. Anyway, it's not our case."

"Thank you, detective," she said, and then she turned to me. "Well, are you ready?"

"That's it?"

"That's it." Miller said.

"For now," Garcia added.

"We may have more questions," Miller added.

Maria handed him her card.

"Please let me know," she said, "if you plan any more interviews."

"Okay."

"Okay?"

"Okay."

It was nearly four A.M. when we got out of there. We walked into the quiet night. It had cooled off, and the stars were thick and bright. The faintest streak of pale blue graced the severing sky in the east.

We walked down the block toward her car—a new two-door Volvo looking all alone and out of place in the empty street.

"I'm sorry I woke you up."

"It's all right," she said, then added, "You'll be sorrier when you see my bill."

"Get in line. I guess I wouldn't have, but the first cop I told my story to only let me get as far as Ryder's disappearance, then he told me to stop, and he put me in back of a squad car to wait for the detectives."

"One body, a cop can handle, two and they start to see a pattern."

"Yeah, so they took me to the station to ask some questions, and I figured I ought to call you."

"Rightly so."

"Oh, by the way," I said, suddenly remembering the owl and digging it out of my shirt pocket, "This is for you."

She looked at it, then pulled the leather thong loose, and slipped it over her head. She was silent for a moment.

"Thank you," she said finally.

"Sure."

She pulled out her key chain and blipped the car alarm. I climbed in and she walked around to the driver's door.

"There's something I didn't tell them," I said as she settled back and the seatbelt folded automatically across her.

"What?" She said, starting the car and swinging around, heading north.

I explained to her about my encounter with Power and the ice cream boys. When I was done, I said, "It still doesn't put me any closer to knowing what's going on."

She was silent for a long time, negotiating her way through the deserted streets of downtown Tucson, past the Temple of Music and Art, the Chicago Store with its wild aboriginal mural, the bus center, and through the Sixth Avenue underpass.

"When I was a young woman," she said at last, "my grandmother told us the stories she had learned from her grandmothers. One of them was about how Coyote stole Sun's tobacco. Do you know that one?"

I shook my head.

"It happened a long time ago—back when Coyote was still living with the People. One day he got bored, so he went to the house of the Sun. Sun wasn't home, but his wife was. And she made a big mistake—she let Coyote in. There's no explaining why she did it. She knew better. But Coyote was a real smooth talker . . ."

She looked at me pointedly.

". . . and he convinced her that he and Sun were good friends, practically like family. Inside the house, Coyote saw Sun's tobacco bag. 'I came to talk to Sun, and have a smoke with him,' Coyote said.

"Sun's wife said that was too bad, because he wouldn't be home for a while. Coyote just smiled. 'Give me a smoke while I'm waiting,' he said. 'Sun won't mind. I'm like a brother to him.'

"My grandmother said that when Coyote spoke to Sun's wife he used the ingratiating tone of a son-in-law."

Again the look. I raised my eyebrows, feigning innocence.

"So Sun's wife handed Coyote the tobacco bag, and he rolled a cigarette. But when Sun's wife turned her back, Coyote took out a bag of his own, and dumped Sun's tobacco into it. Then he took Sun's bag and hung it up where it belonged. Afterward he stretched and yawned. 'Well, it looks like Sun's taking longer than I expected,' Coyote said. 'I guess I won't wait for him after all.' And he left.

"When Sun came home and found his tobacco had been stolen, he was angry, and who would blame him? His wife told him what had happened and he said, 'I'll get Coyote this time.' He went and unhitched Black Wind Horse and saddled him up and went after Coyote. With Black Wind Horse's wings rumbling like thunder, Sun flew after Coyote. He followed the trickster's trail for a long time, but finally he got discouraged and turned back."

"Just like that?" I asked. "He let Coyote get away?"

"Just like that," she said. "Sometimes there comes a point, even when you're chasing someone who has done you wrong, when you have to give up and turn back. Sun came to that point."

I nodded slowly, not entirely convinced. We had been traveling up Fifth Street, and now we turned left on Wilmot, heading toward Tanque Verde.

"Well," she continued, "when Coyote got back to where he was living with the People, they saw the tobacco.

"They asked for just a little bit of tobacco, but he wouldn't give them any. The People held council to figure out what to do. They decided to trick Coyote.

"They figured they could talk Coyote into trading for some of the tobacco. So the People dressed one of the young men of the tribe as a girl, and told him how to act. Then they called Coyote over. 'We've decide to give you a wife,' they said. At first Coyote didn't believe them, but the People kept after him and finally convinced him they were sincere.

"He was so happy he gave all his tobacco to the People, and the People had plenty to smoke."

She pulled to a stop at a red light and was quiet.

"So," I said. "That's it? That's how the story ends?"

"No, of course not. There was still the wedding night."

"Aaah, the wedding night."

"And all through the wedding night," she said, "the boy did just as he'd been told. Every time Coyote tried to come near him, he pushed the trickster away. 'Lie down next to me,' Coyote said. After a while, the boy did—but not very close. 'I want you to lie close,' Coyote said. But the boy pushed him away and wouldn't come closer. It went like that all night."

"Sounds hauntingly familiar," I said.

She glared me into silence.

"Finally, just before dawn, Coyote reached out and grabbed the boy right between the legs. Of course what he found there was an unpleasant surprise. Coyote jumped back and screamed at the boy, 'You're not a girl, get away from me!'

"Coyote ran outside and howled at the people. 'You tricked me, you didn't give me a wife. Give me back my tobacco.'

"But the People wouldn't do it. They'd been up all night smoking tobacco, and they just laughed at Coyote. And that's how the People first got tobacco.

"And when you think about cancer rates on the rez," she said, "maybe Coyote got the last laugh after all."

I nodded slowly. Everything has its price. Still, I just didn't get it.

"What's it got to do with Ryder and Power and the calendar stick?"

"What is the biggest question you have right now, the hardest thing to understand?" he said.

"Easy. What happened to the Ryder's body and the calendar stick? And why was the stick in the box, anyway?"

"When Coyote crawled into the wikiup, he thought he was getting a pretty young bride. He never would have given away his tobacco if he'd known he was being tricked, that he was actually lying down with a boy."

"So?"

"Sometimes," she said, as we pulled into her driveway, "things aren't what they appear to be."

.

Nineteen

Maria's place is a big old ranch house tucked up against the Rincon Mountains. I woke up late, and she was already gone.

Last night seemed like a dream—a nightmare—its immediacy already slipping away. The individual scenes, I remembered; they flickered across my mind like images from a slide show where the tray had been dropped, the slides shoved back in haphazardly. The blood. Her face, her eyes opening with a start, then softening as she spoke. The smoke in the distance. The sirens. The huge neon sign over the Congress exploding as it crumbled into the burning roof. But the images came to me displaced, unanchored, they had no real feel or substance. Surreal.

I stumbled out of bed and padded across cool tiles, down the hall to the kitchen.

My body ached as I moved, my ribs tender from the beating I'd taken, my shoulders tight from all the driving I'd been doing. Jesus, was the girl really dead? Could that have happened? Could and had.

Coffee first, strong and black. Then a couple of slices of toast with butter and jam.

I found the morning paper, unread on the dining room table. I flipped quickly through the first two sections. No mention of the fire. It had probably started after their deadline. It would be in the *Citizen* this afternoon.

I moved into the living room and put a CD on the player. Maria has one of those five-tier, multispeaker systems that is worth more than my Jeep. Like most of her possessions—the big house, the ex-

pensive car—it is, to my anarchistic mind, unnecessary, extravagant
. . . downright sinful. And, every once in a while, it is also very com-
forting.

I sat on the couch, staring out the big plate glass window at the
desert behind her house. Some mornings, wild pigs called peccaries
snuffle up to the house, looking for handouts. Coyotes are common
and, occasionally, when the higher elevations get dry and food is
scarce, a cougar will come down from the mountains for a sip from
the pool.

Apparently I had slept too late—it was already hot out, and time
for smart desert creatures to find a cool place to sleep the day off. But
I sat for a long time, staring up at the craggy mountainside, looking
at the evergreens up there and thinking what a miracle that was. Here,
right in the middle of a furnacelike desert, was an ecosystem you
might find in the Rockies. Just a few thousand feet above us. Hike a
couple of miles, and you might as well be in Telluride. Amazing.

I finished eating, poured myself a second cup of coffee, and then
a third. I couldn't get the French girl out of my head. But I still felt
numb. And I knew, from old experience, that I would go on feeling
just that way, until the sun and the heat crept back into the skin,
down to the bones, and burned it all away.

I was convinced of one thing. Her death and the disappearance
of the body were directly related. It was just too much of a coinci-
dence to swallow. Ryder had been murdered, and now this girl, who
had claimed to have been his girlfriend, had been killed as well.

I had been living the quiet life for a few years now, slow to action,
not seeing the point of jumping in unless I thought my involvement
might have an immediate effect.

But the image of the French girl kept flashing into my brain, the
blood bubbling out of her, the voice a raspy hiss. And then something
else followed. I hadn't known the girl well enough to mourn her. But
she had been something. And now she was nothing. The warm life of
that flesh, cold now, dead.

So that was two people dead, and one a friend.

One thing figured. The trail to Ryder's body would also lead to
whoever killed the French girl.

I decided to make a few phone calls.

First to the *L.A. Times,* where the operator put me through, and Mike picked up right away.

"Hey," he said. "You get my message?"

"I haven't been home."

"Oh. Well, it was easier than I expected. Usually you have to pry information out of these guys like it was a gun clenched in their cold dead hand."

"Nice."

"Thank you. This thing, though, is pretty much a closed case, as far as they're concerned. I mean, they don't have an arrest, so officially the case is open, but unless an informant comes forward—which has got to be considered unlikely—they don't expect to close it."

"Is that good or bad?"

"Good if you want information, bad if you want justice."

"I want peace."

"Through justice, sure. So, anyway, here's the deal. Your guy Ryder Joaquin was the victim of a garden variety drive-by shooting. We have them everyday, although the victim, or target, doesn't always die—not nearly as often as you might think, in fact."

"I don't really have any preconceived notions in that direction."

"The facts of the case, as they appear in the report anyway, are pretty clear. Your pal Ryder was walking down Bringas Boulevard, in the warehouse district. Not a bad neighborhood, really, but not great. Apparently he lived and worked within a few blocks of there—cops found his address on a paycheck stub. Did you know what he was doing, by the way?"

"No, but I'd wondered."

"He was working for an import company called . . . hold on let me find it . . . Marsted. Marsted, Inc."

"So anyway, he's walking down the street, apparently minding his own business—that's what the witnesses reported, and there were a surprising number of them. A truck pulls up alongside of him. That's the way these things usually start. The window rolls down and, whack, your boy is shot in the back, side, and neck. Seven times. The slugs were nine millimeter. The projectile of choice in these things. And again, garden variety. Untraceable."

"Any description of the shooter?"

"No, just the vehicle, which was a late model truck, full-sized, American make with tinted windows. Either red, purple, or blue, depending on which of the witnesses you believe. License plate was white. Means it might be California. Or Ohio, maybe; one of the witnesses said it might have been an Ohio plate.

"How many witnesses, anyway?"

"Five, altogether. For L.A. that's high—although considering the place and the time of day, you can bet maybe six times that many saw it. Actually, this case was a little unusual, considering that one of the witnesses entered the fray."

"Entered the fray?"

"The owner of an electronics store, Korean named Chong Kim. Told the cops he was burned out in the riots. Apparently he's kept himself well-armed since then. When he heard the gunfire in the street, he thought it was a new uprising. Apparently the truck had come to a stop, and the passenger door was opening, someone climbing out—maybe they were going to make sure they finished your friend off, maybe take his wallet, who knows? In any case, they didn't get the chance. Mr. Kim came out of his store firing. I guess that drove them off."

"What kind of weapon?"

"Chinese assault rifle—SKS—confiscated as evidence. Lucky no one got hurt."

"No one but Ryder."

"Yeah . . . I guess that's all of it. If there's anything else I can do for you—"

"As a matter of fact," I said, "there is."

I told him about the French girl and asked if he might not be able to find out what her connection to Ryder was.

"I'll try," he said. "But it might take a while."

"Now that she's dead," I said, "it's probably not all that important. But I'm sure the cops are looking into the connection, too, and that'll involve the L.A. police . . . so anyway it's on your beat."

"Yeah. Listen, I'm sorry about your friend. Looks like he ended up in the wrong place at the wrong time."

"Los Angeles," I said. "Any time."

Next I called Maria. She said she was busy all morning and she was going to be in court until four or so this afternoon. If I wanted a ride back to my place, I'd have to wait until then. I told her I would take a bus.

"Can we meet later?" I asked.

"Sure. How about dinner, around six?"

"Fine."

"Pico de Gallo?"

"Six o'clock."

Next I called information for Los Angeles and got the number for Marsted, Inc.

"Marsted," a female voice answered.

"Personnel, please."

"You're talking to it."

"Oh, well, hello. I'm trying to track down some information on someone who worked for you until recently."

"What for?"

"He was a friend."

"You must mean Ryder."

"How did you know?"

"You said 'was,' and Ryder's the only one I know of who has, well, you know . . ."

"Become past tense."

"It was awful. Ryder was a wonderful guy, just wonderful. Really quiet and all, but there was something, I don't know, magical about him."

"He was a good guy," I said.

"Yup. So what is it you're calling about?"

I debated how much to tell her. Probably the less said the better. I told her I was helping with some of the funeral arrangements, and was having trouble finding all of his friends.

"Have you ever," I asked, "heard of a guy named Sandy Asoza."

"Yup. But you're not going to find him here."

"No?"

"Sandy quit right after Ryder died. I didn't talk to him—which is unusual since this is not a very big place, and I do all the paperwork—but I guess he took it kind of bad about Ryder. I don't blame him. I mean, they were pretty good friends. Anyway, Mr. Martin told me, and had me fill out the paperwork."

"Mr. Martin?"

"Yup. Mr. Martin, and Mr. Stedman. Marsted."

"Oh. Did Sandy leave an address or phone number?"

"Even if he did," she said. "I couldn't give it to you—not over the phone. If you were a collection agency, and you wanted to send a fax . . ."

"Never mind," I said. "But tell me, I'd assumed—I don't know, from the name—that you were a big outfit."

"Just one warehouse, with five or six guys full-time back there. Up front there's just Mr. Martin, Mr. Stedman, and Julia."

"And you?"

"Yup. And me. Speaking of which, I've got to get back to work."

"One last thing," I said. "What exactly does Marsted import?"

"Well, it used to be antiquities and artifacts—really pricey stuff for special collectors. But that's getting harder and harder to find, so they've been expanding to new areas—mostly what you call knock-offs. Replicas from Thailand."

"Replicas?"

"Of whatever's hot at the time. Why buy kachinas from the Indians when you can get them from us at half price?"

"Rhetorical question, right?"

"Yup."

I went to the kitchen and poured myself one last cup of coffee—too much, really, four cups, but I still wasn't feeling any edge from it.

Then I looked up the number for bus route information. This far out of the city, they only showed up about once every hour, and if you missed yours, you were left waiting in the sun.

After I provided the cross streets I was starting from, and my eventual destination, the voice at the other end of the line told me what number bus I needed to take, and where to transfer. It was more complicated than I'd expected, and I had her repeat it a second time, while I jotted it down. The bus stop was about a half-mile away, and the next bus would be there in twenty minutes. Just enough time.

I locked up, and walked out into the heat of the day.

Twenty

It is late June, and the seeds are turning black in the fruit of the saguaros. Time for the harvest. Traditionally, this is the Tohono O'odham New Year. Ryder and I are in a small saguaro harvest camp a few miles west of Tucson. Huge pots boil in fire pits. A makeshift cabinet has been erected in the shade of a palo verde—on the shelves, plastic jugs and buckets, platters and a five-pound bag of sugar, a large container of salt.

Ryder's dark skin glistens in the sun and he smiles as he tells me that some of the fruit will be made into jam and syrup—but most of it is being fermented into nawait, saguaro fruit wine.

Later, in a ceremony that goes on for three days, I stand next to Ryder and drink cup after cup of the bittersweet drink. Ryder is serious. "Going to bring down the clouds," he says. That is what the ceremony is for. To bring the rains for the summer crop. The men will drink and drink—filling up beyond capacity—and then disgorge the brew onto the desert floor.

I continue to drink, but as to this last part I do not think that I will join in.

Then the young man next to me bends over and opens his mouth, flooding the ground. Reflexively I follow suit. It is painful. My eyes water, my nose and throat sting. I cough hard as I fight to stand up straight. I look over at Ryder. He is wiping his mouth. I feel the pained look in my own eyes. He smiles. I am learning the ways of his people.

ig Jack Woolf is a man of nearly mythical proportions. He stands seven feet tall, with a barrel chest and huge belly. His forehead, which grows a little longer every year as his hairline retreats, is a maze of craggy lines. Between his eyes is a dark, round mole the size of a button, and when his brows come together in a look of intense concentration, you cannot help but wonder for a moment if he isn't about to turn you into a toad.

Woolf's appearance sometimes seems to cause him consternation—he is, after all, a gentle soul trapped in the body of a giant. He is also the Southwest's great folklorist. The history of the land runs in his veins. If anyone could answer a riddle about a calendar stick, it was Big Jack.

I watched as Woolf paced slowly back and forth on the low stage at the front of the small lecture hall, his hands clasped behind his back.

Having emerged from the bus, victorious, I had walked two blocks and recovered my vehicle from where I'd parked it. The shattered windshield would have to wait. I drove by the gutted wreckage of the Congress, cordoned off by yellow tape. Workers were already starting to put up a temporary fence. I turned north, and then made a right, and after a couple of blocks started looking for a place to park. I got lucky, finding one just a block and a half from the huge volcanic rock pillars at the main gate to the university.

I checked Jack's office, found it locked, the room beyond the opaque glass dark.

The receptionist in the office of the Humanities department told me he was teaching a class. I asked for directions.

"Back out to the staircase, down one floor. It's right underneath us."

I had slipped quietly into the classroom, finding a chair in the back row.

Now, I looked around at Jack's students. There were about fifty in all, in a lecture hall that was designed to hold twice that number. Most of them were down front, crowded around the stage, listening intently to Woolf's controlled, sonorous voice—more like the voice of a veteran disc jockey than that of a college professor—as he told them about La Corua, the giant serpent that lives underground and protects the desert springs.

"When the Corua is killed, the spring dries up . . ." Woolf was saying.

Except for a couple of slackers in the back, the students were rapt and a few of them bent over their notebooks, scribbling furiously.

I sat back and made myself comfortable, taking in the lecture. The clock hit the top of the hour, and Woolf finished up.

I waited till most of the class had shuffled out, then made my way down to the stage, where the big man was standing at the podium, stuffing his papers into an old leather satchel. As I hopped up onto the stage he looked up.

"Grayson!" he said. Other than my mother and her sister, he is the only person who calls me by that name. For most people it would seem overly formal, but he makes it sound perfunctory. "How's the botanical trade?"

"Interesting," I said. "Consistently interesting."

A young man with stringy blond hair approached us. He had been one of the scribblers, working furiously throughout the lecture to get every word into his notes.

"Excuse me, Dr. Woolf," he said.

"What can I do for you, Paul?"

"I have this friend who grew up in Greenland—anyway, for his master's project at NYU he translated this—" He handed Woolf a thick, typed manuscript. "Ice Tales. I thought you might want a copy."

"Thank you. I'll read it this evening."

The young man nodded shyly and walked away.

"Sort of like giving the teacher an apple," I said after he was out of earshot.

"So how are you?" the big man asked casually as he stuffed the manuscript in with the rest of his papers. Then he looked up. I must have looked pretty bad, because his voice lost its light tone, suddenly grew concerned. "Damn it, man, are you all right? What's wrong?"

At first I'd intended to simply ask him about the calendar stick, but I ended up telling him all of it, from the start—the road back from L.A., and stopping at Why for gas. I told him about coming out and finding the body gone, and then tracking down Uncle Charlie and

Theresa Joaquin, and meeting the French girl. Then I explained about Power's involvement, and his missing calendar stick.

And finally, I told him about the night before, the Congress fire, and the French girl's death—and the word she'd spoken, a word I didn't understand, something that sounded like "lehzaytwal."

When I was done, he shook his head slowly.

"I'm sorry about your friend," he said.

I shrugged.

"Right offhand I can't think of anything like that. There are a few calendar sticks in the State Museum, maybe one or two in private collections. None like what you're looking for."

"Well, hell."

"I wish I could be more helpful."

"I'll just have to keep digging."

"After all these years," Woolf said, "there's one thing I've learned about the history of this region—no matter how long and hard you look, you may not find what you're after. But don't be dejected, you'll at least come up with some interesting substitutes."

"You want to go get a beer, maybe a cup of coffee?"

"I would love to," Woolf said. "But unfortunately I can't. Bill Buckmaster and a camera crew from *Arizona Illustrated* will be here any minute. I am to be interviewed about my new book."

"Must be tough," I said, "to be a star."

I said good-bye, and turned to go.

I was halfway up the aisle when his voice stopped me.

"Grayson. Grayson, this French woman—are you sure it was just one word she spoke at the end?"

"I'm not sure of anything, except that I'm in way over my head."

He smiled.

"Well, it doesn't have anything to do with a calendar stick, but maybe I can answer one of your questions. Repeat the word," Woolf said.

As accurately as I could, I made the sounds she had made, nonsensical as they were to me.

Woolf nodded.

"It sounds to me like she was saying *les étoiles*—"

"That's right—"

"Which is French, of course. It translates as *the stars.*"

"The stars?"

"You say she opened her eyes the moment before?"

". . . and looked right up at the night sky."

"Could be."

"The stars. Well, to tell you the truth, it's a little bit of a letdown."

"Maybe," Woolf said. "On the other hand, there might be more to it than that."

"Tell me."

"You're familiar with San Xavier?"

"Sure."

Like anyone in town, I had been to the famous mission—the White Dove of the Desert—and because it was on O'odham land, and played a central role in the lives of some of the People, I had read the histories—including one written by Woolf.

"Do you know the statue behind the altar?"

"Saint Francis, right?"

"Yes. And above him, Our Lady of Immaculate Conception. And above her, the old man himself, God the Father."

"I didn't realize."

"Well, these things don't come with numbers. There is a story that goes with those statues—a story about The Stars—though in the story they're known by their Spanish name, Las Estrellas.

"Padre Kino was the first to suggest a mission on the site now occupied by San Xavier. He visited the native village called Bac in the late 1600s, and made plans for a mission there. But the plans weren't carried out until nearly a hundred years later—when Fray Velderrain started work on the project. When Velderrain died, Fray Llorenz took over and finished the project—all but the east tower, which was never completed, and remains unfinished to this day. Like most of the Spanish colonial missions, San Xavier was built by native laborers— the O'odham. We know quite a bit about the building of the mission, but there is more that is unknown or half-known—the oral traditions, passed down generation to generation by a people who have lived on this land since before Columbus touched ground at San Salvador. Why, for instance, did Kino make his plans, but not build his mission?"

I shrugged. But he wasn't really looking for an answer, and he plowed on without stopping.

"Some say it was time constraint—Kino was driven to push farther north and west, to save more souls, to explore the uncharted reaches of New Spain's northern frontier. Others say it was money. He didn't have the funds to build the mission, and the church wouldn't help him."

"But what does that have to do with the stars—Las Estrellas?"

"Everything. There's one oral tradition, usually overlooked—possibly because historians find it so incredible, or perhaps because they don't dig deeply enough. Lumholtz mentions it in his smaller third book of travels, and Pfeffercorn made note of it in the margin of one of his diaries, but otherwise I've not seen reference to it anywhere. It is the story of Las Estrellas."

Just then the door to the room opened, and three young men burst in, talking loudly among themselves. They stopped a few steps past the threshold and looked around at the empty room, then at each other. Finally one of them got a bright look on his face.

"Wrong room!" he said.

"Wrong floor," the second one said.

"Dude!"

Then they disappeared back the way they had come.

I raised my eyebrows at Woolf, but he never missed a beat.

"Tradition has it that Kino wanted to build the mission, but he didn't have the money. So he appealed secretly to the Queen of Spain for funds. She agreed to help him.

"She removed five jewels from her crown. Three emeralds and two diamonds. Las Estrellas. She had a jeweler replace them with fakes. Secretly, she sent the stones to Kino. The padre received the gems, and put them in a strong box which he hid at the spot where he planned to build the mission. A week later, he rode to Magdalena for the dedication of a new chapel to his patron saint, Francisco Xavier. Kino fell suddenly ill, and a few days later he was dead. There are those who say he was poisoned—poisoned by thieves after Las Estrellas. His bones, you know, were unearthed by archaeologists in Mexico thirty years ago—he'd been buried under the chapel at Magdalena—and they can be seen there today.

"Fifty years later the Jesuits were expelled from New Spain, by order of the king. The reasons aren't entirely clear, but it has always been suggested that the Jesuits were hoarding silver and gold, mined for them by the Indians.

"According to the legend, if thieves did in fact kill Kino, they did not find the stones. They weren't discovered until Fray Llorenz—a Franciscan—began the final phase of the building.

"And it's said that when San Xavier was built, a crown was made to fit atop the statue of Our Lady of the Immaculate Conception. The crown had five settings, five large settings. The settings, of course, were for Las Estrellas. But the gems were stolen, of course, before the crown was ever placed on Our Lady's head. At the time they were stolen, the mission was nearly completed. Fray Llorenz halted work immediately—leaving the east tower unfinished. And as the story goes, the Franciscan declared that the tower would not be completed until the gems were returned."

He was quiet for a few moments.

Finally I asked, "And? . . ."

"And, of course, there is no evidence that any such crown ever *actually* existed, or that any such jewels ever existed. Just like with all of the Spanish silver and gold that is supposed to be buried out there, subtle signs, hints and markings seem to appear, then vanish, and the treasure itself is never found.

"No one has ever found the material riches they looked for in this arid land, Grayson. Not Coronado, not the Earps, not the seekers of the Dutchman's gold. The real treasure here is the land and its people, their rich and fantastic tales, their beliefs, their holy places."

Twenty-one

Pico de Gallo is on South Sixth Avenue, near the freeway. It's not much to look at, the kind of whitewashed taqueria most people pass by without a second glance, but it serves the best Mexican food in town. The menu is limited to whatever's on hand—carne asada, chicken, sometimes fish—but the food is always fresh, well-cooked, and made from scratch. In the old days, the woman at the stove made the tortillas by hand while your food was cooking, patting them out with a skillful flip-flap-flap motion. But word has gotten out—it always does—and now they're just a little too busy, so they press them in cooking irons. The price of progress.

I waited at a small table up front, reading the afternoon paper and keeping one eye on the door, watching for Maria.

The *Citizen* had a big story about the fire—a color photo splashed across the page, and a large headline—Blaze Destroys Congress.

According to the article, the fire started when a table of large chafing dishes was overturned. Witnesses reported a scuffle involving a woman and two men just before the fire broke out—it was thought that the scuffle might have resulted in the fire.

There was a sidebar reporting the murder of a woman near the railroad tracks. The woman's identity was unknown. Police did not say whether she was the same woman involved in the scuffle at the hotel, but they were investigating the possibility.

The person who found the dying woman was reported only as "a local man."

I mulled the articles over as I read the rest of the paper, glancing at the door every moment or two.

I was so surprised when Ben and Jerry walked in that at first it didn't register. But it was really them, the ice cream brothers, stumbling in like a pair of sea turtles suddenly thrust onto the floor of the House of Representatives.

The sloppy one was wearing a baggy pair of jeans with many creases across the crotch, and the same Hawaiian shirt he'd had on the last time I saw him. Or one just like it.

The short man wore a tan cotton suitcoat and pants that would have looked good on a senator's aide as he walked into the lobby of the Hart Building in D.C., but seemed out of place on his stocky frame. He wore a colorful bow tie at the throat of his lavender shirt.

They spotted me right away and walked up to my table.

"Hello, darling," the short man said.

"Ben, right? Or is it Jerry?"

"I'm Ben," the sloppy one said, dropping into the chair across from me.

"So that makes you . . . ?"

"Shut up, asshole," Jerry said.

"Or, to be precise," Ben said, "we have something to tell you, and it would be in your best interest to listen."

"In the car," Jerry hissed.

"Look," I said, "I'd like to invite you guys to join me, but I'm expecting company."

"You just had a change of plans," Jerry said. "Let's go."

"Like I said—"

"There's two ways to do this," the short man said. "The easy way, and the way I'll enjoy."

"To be precise," Ben added, "why make a mess?"

With that, Jerry moved behind me and stuck what I assumed to be his automatic into the area just above my left kidney.

"Shall we?"

"How long is this going to take?"

"Could be a while."

I stood, pushing my chair back. As I rose, I felt the pressure removed, and I figured he had tucked the gun back under his coat, because as we moved to the door, he pulled up alongside of me, grabbing me by the elbow, while with his other hand he waved casually to the man behind the cash register who was eying all three of us suspiciously.

"Everything okay, Napoleon?" he asked.

"Fine, Nando," I answered. "I was going to meet Maria, but I have to run an errand. When she shows up, would you tell her I had to leave and I'll call her later?"

"Okay. You sure it's all right?"

"Fine."

I followed them out to the parking lot and Ben opened the back door of the Cherokee. I climbed in. This time he climbed in next to me.

They were silent as we pulled out of the parking lot and drove to the freeway entrance.

"Mind telling me where we're going?"

Silence.

Jerry drove a couple of miles west, then exited onto Interstate 19. We crossed the bridge over the dry Santa Cruz riverbed. There was a time when it flowed year-round, and flooded a mile wide. No more.

Jerry took the Ajo exit and cruised slowly through traffic to Mission Road. At Mission we headed south, and soon we were on O'odham land.

The O'odham are not really one tribe. Traditionally, the village was the central force of O'odham society. And in old times, the People could be told apart by the number of villages they lived in. Tohono O'odham, the People of the Desert, were Two Villagers. They had a summer village in the low country, where they cultivated bean fields and flood irrigated when the monsoons came, and a winter home on higher land, near a permanent spring. Further north lived the Akimal O'odham, or One Villagers. They lived along the Salt and the Gila rivers—in the area now dominated by the city of Phoenix. Then there were the Hia-Ced O'odham, or Sand People. They were known as No Villagers, and thought of as nomads. Their home was the harshest desert in the Southwest—the shifting, barren region from El Gran Desierto to the Colorado Delta.

Now, there is a fourth classification. The River People. They live on the banks of the dry Santa Cruz, by San Xavier Mission.

132

Eventually we turned again, then Jerry pulled off the road into the dirt lot across from San Xavier.

"Let's go," the short man said, and we climbed out of the Cherokee, walking back across the blacktop to the mission.

Inside, San Xavier is laid out in the traditional mission style—the building runs in the shape of a cross, with the entrance at the foot, the altar at the top, and recesses at either arm.

Power sat halfway down the center row of pews, his sloped shoulders and the great orb of his head visible above the bench back.

Except for the two of us, and Ben and Jerry at the door, the church was empty.

I walked slowly down the left aisle and slid into the pew next to him.

The old man was staring forward, his head tilted slightly back. I followed his gaze beyond the altar, to the statue above Saint Francis.

For a long time Power was silent, then he sighed.

"She is beautiful, isn't she?"

"Our Lady," I said. "Yes, she is."

"Perfection," he said.

"Almost," I replied.

"Almost?"

"She would look better with a crown on her head, wouldn't she?"

He smiled.

"So you know about Las Estrellas?"

"Some of it," I said.

"Well, perhaps I should have told you in the first place and saved you the time and effort of finding out. But what man would? We old men cherish our secrets. And we are loath to let them go."

"Some people are that way about their guns."

"What? Oh, yes, I suppose so. Guns have never interested me. It is always good to have a couple of people working for you who know how to use them. Brute force. But it has to be controlled. I have always been interested in other things—my collections all contain unusual objects. Objects more powerful than weapons."

"Right," I said. "Thing is, I'm supposed to meet someone, so unless you've got something specific in mind, I don't really have time for this."

"Oh, you have time. More time than you imagine. More than I. What did you find out about Las Estrellas, Mister Napoleon?"

"Enough," I answered. "Frankly, I'm beginning to think the whole thing is pretty silly. All except the part where my friend's body disappears and his family can't breathe without wondering what the hell has happened to him. And it's all over what? Some adolescent legend about lost treasure that we both know isn't real?"

"Oh, it's real, Mister Napoleon, it is very, very real. And I do not intend to let it slip through my fingers."

"Good luck," I said, and got up to leave. I moved to the end of the pew and turned, heading for the door.

"Mister Napoleon!" the old man called after me. And when I turned he was holding his left hand high in the air, the fist clenched.

He opened the fist. A stone rolled out of his hand, falling to the end of a leather strap. The small, white rock, carved in the shape of an owl, swung back and forth by his elbow.

"I'm not through yet," he said.

I recognized the carving immediately and turned toward him.

"She said you would recognize this."

The rage rose up in me like an animal—a monstrous beast screaming through my mind.

I moved quickly to him, snagged the carving from the air.

"Where is she?"

"Safe."

I lunged forward and grabbed his throat with one meaty hand.

"Where . . . is . . . she?" I applied pressure to the throat, feeling it squish easily in my hand, like thick clay.

Out of the corner of my eye I saw Jerry running down the aisle toward us. Crouched low and moving fast, he had the gun out, held close to one hip.

I swung around to the other side of the old man, letting go of his throat and dropping the fetish, wrapping one arm around his neck, under his jaw, the hand over his shoulder. The other arm I pushed against the base of his neck, locking the hand against my own bicep.

As Jerry neared, I twisted the old man around, making a shield of him, and putting a little pressure against the neck.

"One quick snap," I said. "Is all it will take."

Jerry was at the aisle now, moving toward us, shifting back and forth like a snake, the gun out in front of him.

"Tell him to stop," I said quietly into the old man's ear.

Power reached up in the air with one thin arm, held up a shaky hand.

"One moment, Jerry," he said.

The short man froze. I shifted again, putting as much of the old man between myself and Jerry as possible.

"Now," I said to the old man, "he puts the gun down on the bench and backs away."

"The pistol, Jerry. Set it down," he said. "I think that will be all, then. You can wait in the car."

Jerry backed out of the pew and started up the aisle toward the door. When he'd gotten far enough, I pushed Power away from me and stepped past him toward the gun. I was reaching for it with my right hand when the lights went out.

I came to with the sloppy man sitting to the left of me and Power on my right.

"Well, that wasn't bad now, was it?" Power said, looking at his watch. "Less than two minutes."

He had red marks on his neck where I'd choked him, but his face was calm and composed.

I felt breath at my ear, and then Jerry's voice, barely more than a whisper from behind.

"One fucking thing, ratshit, try one fucking thing," he poked the gun barrel against my spinal cortex, "and I will gladly remove your brains."

Ben just stared ahead quietly. From the smug look on his face it was easy enough to guess who had hit me from behind.

He must have snuck up while I was talking to his partner. I realized I had kept the old man on my left side, blocking my view of the other aisle, giving the sloppy one a perfect shield. *Not good, Napoleon, not good.*

"Okay," I said to Power, "no more tricks. But let me tell you one thing. If you've hurt her, you'd better have him kill me now—"

"I know, Mister Napoleon, because you will come after me if it's the last thing, and so on . . . Really I don't think there's any need for all this." He rubbed his neck gently. "I am an old man. I don't want to hurt anybody. She is safe, unharmed. What's more, she has no idea who has taken—how shall we say it—possession of her. She is a lovely woman, Mister Napoleon, a lovely woman. I won't harm her, unless—"

"No unless."

Jerry clocked me in the back of the head with his gun barrel.

"Unless," Power went on, "you refuse to help me. You see, I am quite certain you have certain information—information that will lead me to Las Estrellas."

"What?"

"You recently met a certain young French woman, did you not?"

"Caroline?"

"Her name is not Caroline, it is Julia."

"Julia?"

"Oui. She worked for the people from whom I was to buy the gems. Was. Actually, I paid half in advance. And who wouldn't? We are talking about a lifelong goal, suddenly within reach. Who would have thought, so late in life?

"I have been searching for Las Estrellas for nearly sixty years. I have seen duplicates, and they are indeed magnificent. Five stones. Three emeralds, and two diamonds, each roughly the size of an egg. Do you understand the implication?"

I opened my mouth to speak but he cut me off.

"I think not. The emeralds themselves are worth millions of dollars. But the diamonds. They are the real prize. Two stones, each the size of the Hope. They are known as Los Gemellos. The Twins. You see, Mister Napoleon, they are identical."

"I guess they're worth even more," I said.

"Priceless. Truly priceless. Only a handful of corporations in the world could afford them at auction—and perhaps three individuals.

"I first learned of them in Paris, not long after my run-in with Hemingway."

I started to shift uncomfortably, and I saw Ben glance at his watch.

"It's a long story," Power said shortly. "And I won't bore you with it. But in Spain I learned that the story of Las Estrellas was indeed

136

true, and that few knew it. I have hunted for them since. In the last ten years—since my fourth wife died—I've intensified my search. I've employed several individuals, and have had standing offers with a handful of discreet firms.

"Finally, a few weeks ago, Las Estrellas turned up. The import company your French girl worked for located them in Chechnya. How they got there is a mystery. What matters is that they were in the hands of a private party who was selling off sixty years of Soviet secrets in hopes of funding the new revolution. This time, I believe, they are fighting for freedom, rather than demagoguery.

"I agreed to pay a huge sum. And half of it was necessary in advance. For me, this has required a vast restructuring of my wealth. Such an endeavor is always delicate. Money—big money—is only safe if it is left with other big money. Together they grow. I have put myself in a tenuous position. But it was a necessary, worthwhile risk. You see, I will not have to worry about money once the gems are mine. It is worth the bulk of my fortune to acquire them. No. It is worth everything. For they have been my life's purpose.

"You would think that the transportation of such an item would be easy. Unfortunately, it was bungled. They were smuggled first out of the former Soviet Union, then to Thailand. There they were inserted into the hollowed-out center of a fake calendar stick. The stick was waiting to pass through customs at the warehouse of the company that acquired the gems for me—Marsted.

"Your friend Ryder Joaquin was working in that warehouse. Somehow, he was allowed into the room where the calendar stick was stored. Apparently he and the French girl were more than friends. The horrible thing about all this is that it was a simple mistake. Your friend didn't realize that the calendar stick was a fake—a hollowed-out fake with the gems inside—and when he saw it in the vault, he thought it was something that should not be sold. He couldn't stand by and let them sell something that by rights belonged to his people. He grabbed the stick, and bolted, intending to head for home.

"They caught up to him that afternoon on the street and shot him down. They would have recovered the stick then, except that the merchants of Los Angeles are now apparently better armed than some of the criminal element. They were driven off by a shop owner, the calendar stick taken into custody by the police.

"Another opportunity was missed when they tried to bribe the police officer at the evidence room to let them look for the stick. They arrived too late. The stick had already been packed up with your friend's other possessions—in the funeral box.

"Meantime you arrived and took possession of the body. Now, I am somewhat concerned. These gentlemen—Martin and Stedman—they have no loyalty to me. They have half of my money, which I am working diligently to regain. But I think that despite the incredible price I was willing to pay for the stones, they did not realize what they had on their hands. Now they do. And I'm afraid they have found another buyer—one who is willing to double or triple my offer. I can't even attempt to match such a figure.

"So, if they find the gems before I do, I am in a great deal of trouble. They know I no longer trust them. And having discovered the true value of the stones, they won't worry about a little thing like their reputation. We are talking about richness beyond most men's conception."

"Why are you telling me all of this?"

"Because, Mister Napoleon, I have something you want. And I expect you to find what I want. Certainly you are the man in the best position to recover Las Estrellas and make the trade. I have others working on it as well, but I have decided that you are the most promising and I don't think you will fail me."

"And if I do?"

"Don't talk of such things, Mister Napoleon, don't talk of such things. Find them, and do it quickly. I said I was in a tenuous financial position? It is worse than that. I am in a state of fiscal crisis. I need assurance by the start of business tomorrow, or frankly, I will be ruined." He looked at his watch. "Shall we say twelve hours? You have twelve hours, Mister Napoleon. Find Las Estrellas."

Twenty-two

The phone was ringing as I walked in the door. I snatched it off the hook.

"Hello."

"Gray? Gray Napoleon?" A woman's voice.

"Yes."

"I don't know if you'll remember me. My name is Katy Crimson. I'm Sharon Spelling's sister. Sharon's a friend of Maria's. I met you at a party for Native Seeds—the one where Leslie Silko and Jim Harrison read? Gary Nabhan too. Oh, you don't remember, do you?"

I searched my brain for the night in question. Pinned it down. I remembered talking to Sharon, and a woman approaching us.

"Blond?" I said. "About five-five, with tortoiseshell glasses?"

"You do remember. It must be nice to have a brain that works like that. Mine certainly doesn't. Everywhere at once, that's me. Of course I did remember *your* name. It's so unusual."

"So I'm told."

"Well, like I said, it may be nothing—I hope I'm not interrupting anything—"

"Actually, it has been a long day—and I'm just getting started."

"Then I'll get right to the point. I work at St. Mary's Hospital, I guess you don't remember that, as a night nurse?

"Sure," I said, not remembering.

"It's the strangest thing," she continued. "There's man out here—a new patient. The thing is, he keeps saying your name."

Twenty-three

He's right down here," she said.

She had told me where to park, which floor to take the elevator to, and I had driven through downtown and under the freeway to the foot of the black hills where the white hospital rose against the sky.

I recognized her immediately at the nurse's station. She spoke softly as she guided me down the hallway.

"I'm really sorry to have bothered you," she said. "I hope I wasn't wrong to do it. We don't know his identity—he was brought in this morning. He's suffering from exposure. Heat stroke."

"How bad?"

"Bad. We see cases like this regularly—people who have gotten lost out there for a day or two—but this is the worst I've ever seen."

We turned a corner and walked down another hallway.

"Anyway, we don't know who he is, and it doesn't look like he's going to live. In addition to the heatstroke, he suffered a head injury. Lost a lot of blood when he could least afford to. Lucky he lived at all."

She stopped in front of a door.

"He's mostly been unconscious, but when he came to earlier, he repeated a few words over and over. Mostly, your name. The morning nurse didn't really think anything of it. She figured it was just part of the delirium. She didn't think it was unusual for him to say Napoleon, or gray Napoleon. After all, he is a Frenchman."

We stepped into a small anteroom, and she pulled gloves and boots and a surgical gown from a row of shelves.

"You'll have to put these on," she said.

I tugged the sterile outfit on over my clothes, she pushed the door open, and I walked in.

"Do you recognize him?" she asked.

"I don't think so." It was hard to tell. The man was lying on his back in the hospital bed, the sheet pulled up to his chest. His face was a deep, unhealthy red, and skin was peeling from it in great patches. His lips were cracked and swollen, run through with bloody lines. Large areas of raw skin glistened on his neck and shoulders, apparently places where huge blisters had swollen then popped.

His head was wrapped in gauze, tubes ran down the sides of his face and disappeared into his nose. I.V.'s dripped silently into his arms.

I moved closer.

"I have work to do," Katy said. "If you want to stay for a little while, you can. If he wakes up, he might recognize you. Maybe you can get his name out of him. Maybe."

I sat in a chair on the far side of the bed, watching his chest rise and fall in a ragged rhythm.

I looked at him closely. The ravages of the desert can change a man's appearance greatly. The skin swells and stretches, the features deform. But I was sure I didn't know this man. I wondered how she knew he was French, but then the words came out in a shaky whisper, the voice thickly accented, and I understood.

"Napoleon," he whispered. "Napoleon."

I leaned back in my chair, not sure how to react.

"Napoleon," he said again. Then his chest sank and he went back to the ragged breathing. Hallucination or not, the effort was costing him.

I leaned forward, spoke close to his ear.

"I'm Napoleon."

Nothing.

"I'm Gray Napoleon."

The breathing hitched, then started. A deep, soft rattle down in there somewhere, then the voice.

"Napoleon. Gray Napoleon."

"Right here," I said. "I'm right here with you."

Again his chest hitched, then fell, hitched then fell. His mouth worked up and down a little.

"Five crosses," he said. Then settled back to breathing.

I sat for a long time, waiting. But there was nothing more. After a while Katy poked her head in the door. She raised her eyebrows. I shook my head and rose from the chair. I followed her out of the room and began stripping off the sterile garb.

"Well?" she said.

"No name," I said, tugging the smock over my head. "Sorry. Is he going to be all right?"

"Doubtful. The head injury really complicated things. He may have been hit by a car, no one's really sure. All we know is he came out of the desert on I-8, and a passing motorist called the sheriff's on her cellular."

"I-8?"

"Somewhere west of Gila Bend. They medevaced him here because we specialize in extreme exposure cases."

"What'll happen to him?" The left bootie snagged on my shoelaces and I yanked at it, finally pulled it free.

She shrugged. "Have to wait and see."

"If his condition changes," I said, slipping off the trousers, "will you call me?"

"Okay. If it changes."

"One way or the other," I rolled the clothes in a bundle and handed them to her.

"Okay."

Twenty-four

I headed crosstown, passing under the Interstate and driving past the university.

I thought Power would be true to his word. It wouldn't gain him anything to harm Maria and it would open up all kinds of possible complications.

I wished I had gotten the call from the hospital before the meeting at San Xavier. Because now I had one more question for the old man. With the answer to that one question, I thought, I just might prove him right, and be the one to find his precious gems. But I only knew one way to get in touch with him.

I turned left on Campbell and headed north, past the shops in bookstore row, and up into the foothills.

I had crossed the bridge and was easing through the first curve past the riverbed when I noticed the truck in my rearview mirror.

Actually, once I noticed, it occurred to me that he'd been back there for a while. It was red, a late model GMC. Big curving wheel wells, fat tires, jacked way up, with a row of daylighters running across the roll bar.

I thought back. It seemed to me that the same truck, or one very like it had been parked near the Land Cruiser when I came out of the hospital. Dark tinted windows, I remembered, couldn't see inside.

I looked back in the mirror carefully. There were two or three people crowded into the vehicle.

I pushed gently down on the gas, gaining speed as I came to the hill that marked the beginning of the twisting turning rise into the foothills.

I gained a little space on the truck, then I was climbing, cutting left through a turn, the yellow signs with wide black arrows flashing by on my right.

The Land Cruiser chugged a little at the top of the hill, the valves chattering. The motor caught and I was skittering through the next curve, then straightening out.

The truck was on me quickly. Its big V-8 engine accelerating effortlessly.

Shit, I thought, I've had enough of this lately. But I was already barreling through another turn, clutching the steering wheel hard, fighting through the bend.

I thought I had negotiated the turn successfully when I felt them nudge my rear bumper.

It happened so quickly I didn't have time to react. The Land Cruiser was already leaning far into the turn, the tires hardly gripping blacktop, and the little bump was all it took.

Suddenly I was floating around, the back end swinging sideways, the road disappearing on my left, scrub brush and dirt and rocks looming up on my right.

Then the wheel hit something, maybe a barrel cactus, maybe a big rock; the Land Cruiser's center of gravity was blown, and the vehicle was rolling onto its side, grinding into the desert floor.

Twenty-five

I came to upside down, hanging from my seat belt. After a moment, I realized I hadn't really been unconscious, just shaken. Hard. I moved my head around gently. I looked up, or rather down, at the ground. A jagged rock, the size of a bowling ball was right under my head, inches away.

The roll bar, I could see, had given a little, then held. The windshield had been smashed flat and the steel frame was resting over my thighs.

Close call.

Then I felt hands reaching in, working the seat belt loose, pulling me out as I fell to the ground.

I must have been worse off than I realized, because I could offer up no resistance as the two big men—dark tans, shiny black hair—dragged me toward the truck.

A couple of other cars had stopped, and a small man with gray hair was climbing out of one, motioning the woman in the passenger seat to stay there.

"Is he okay?" he asked as he approached.

"Got to get him to a hospital," one of the big men said, as they lifted me into the truck.

I tried to speak, to protest, but only mumbled incoherently.

"Maybe you should wait for an ambulance," gray hair said.

"Can't take the chance," the other man said, as he climbed in next to me. "Why don't you wait for the police and tell them we went to the hospital."

"Well, I'm not sure, I—" gray hair said.

The big man closed the door as his partner started the truck, gunned the engine, and backed out onto the street.

They headed up into the hills first, then turned right, toward the mountains. The car hummed along on the smooth blacktop of Sunrise.

"He don't look so good," the one on my right said.

"He'll live," the driver said. Then I closed my eyes, and quit caring.

It was dark when I woke up, and not really cool, but not hot anymore.

I could see the stars overhead through the tree branches. My head hurt fiercely. For a while I attempted to go back to sleep, but the pain kept pulling me to the surface. Finally I gave up trying. Instead, I concentrated on breathing as deeply and smoothly as possible.

After a while I opened my eyes again. The stars had shifted. The sliver moon was up.

I heard voices, talking somewhere off to my left. I tried moving my head. A bolt of pain shot through it. Then a wave of nausea rose in my throat. In a moment things settled and I looked in the direction of the voices.

I could make out the curve of steel, and cargo hooks, and I realized I was in the bed of a truck.

Truck?

Then it came back to me slowly—I remembered being pushed off the road, and dragged from the vehicle, that was all.

The voices were still talking, muted and low. Too low to make out clearly, anyway.

Finally I pulled myself over to the side of the truck bed. The pain was bad for a minute, then it faded.

I eased myself up a little, so I was sitting with my back against the wheel-well, my head pressed against the hard, cool steel of the rail.

"Well," one voice said, "I guess it's time. Let's get him out of there."

There was some shuffling, then the voices were coming from my left, at the rear of the truck.

"He's up. That saves a little effort."

"Let's go, Romeo," the other added.

I looked over, and it was the two from earlier. No surprise there. The white teeth of the driver shone as he smiled in the darkness.

"Hup-hup," the other one said.

I dragged myself along the rail of the truck to the rear end. They dropped the gate.

"Do his hands," the driver said, and the other man walked around to the passenger door of the truck. He opened it and light spilled out into the night.

After a moment he returned with a roll of duct tape.

"Put your hands out," he said to me. I stuck them in front of me and he pinched them together. Then he started the roll and wrapped the tape around my wrists in six or seven passes.

They grabbed me by the shoulders and hefted me out, then dragged me stumbling through the trees to a place where a few big rocks had been pulled into a circle. In the middle, a small fire was burning in a pit. I wondered why they needed it. It certainly wasn't to keep warm.

They let go and I sat down hard.

"Okay," the driver said, "just keep your eyes open. I'll be back as soon as I can."

"Yeah?" the other one said. "Well, don't fuck around. I don't like it so much out here."

"Anybody comes, just take care of things. And keep him quiet."

"Yeah."

I sat there for a while, my back against a tree trunk. I looked up at the skeleton branches—*Cercidium floridum,* blue palo verde—so I was in high desert.

The big man sat on one of the rocks, close to the fire—too close considering that it wasn't cold out. Every few minutes he looked around nervously, then he would stare at the ground near the fire, or at me. City boy, I thought, a dude. Spooked by the emptiness of the darkened desert. Needed the fire for company.

"You Martin?" I asked.

He shook his head. "Hell no, that was Martin," he said, nodding to where the truck had been.

"So you're Stedman."

He shook his head again.

"Unh-uh."

"Who, then?"

"You don't want to know."

"Oh."

"They call me Cobra."

"Oh."

"Like the movie."

"Oh." I had no idea what he was talking about.

We were both quiet for a while.

"So, can I leave now?" I asked at last.

He guffawed. Then he said seriously, "You can't go nowhere."

"Right."

"What it is," he said, "is this—you seem like an okay guy. A little fucked up probably, but who isn't?"

I couldn't argue with him there.

"Martin, he don't really run things. He thinks he does, but he don't. Stedman's the man. We've had a man watchin' our boy at the hospital since this morning. Very low profile—your nurse friend, she doesn't even know he exists.

"Now, he seen you in there talking to our boy. Like I said, we been watchin' our boy. So Martin, he's on his way right now to pick up the Man from the airport—"

"Not the boy?"

"The boy's in the hospital."

"With the man."

"Our man's at the hospital—with the boy."

"Then who's on the plane?"

He looked at me long and hard.

"Stedman."

"The Man."

"Right. Now he and Martin's gonna talk things over. They'll check on our boy's condition. If he's better, we don't need you. If he ain't, who knows?"

"Can I ask you one question?"

"Shoot."

"Do you know the French girl?"

"Yeah, I knew her." His teeth shone in the firelight as he smiled a big, nasty smile. "Knew her real good."

"Well here's my question—did she know your boy?"

He nodded slowly, still smiling.

"You know," he said, "you're a pretty smart guy. I never would have figured that out."

"What was he, boyfriend?"

"Brother. How'd you guess she knew him?" he asked.

"Well, it just went to figure, after all he—" I caught myself. I'd been about to tell him that their boy spoke French. But on second thought, I didn't figure it would be a good idea for them to know he had talked to me. "It just figured, that's all."

The smile left his face and his eyes narrowed to slits.

"That's okay," he said. "Keep it to yourself. When Stedman gets here there's two ways it can go—either we need you, or we don't. Either way you're going to answer all our questions."

An hour later, I was sitting in the same spot, with my eyes pressed nearly closed, watching the big man by the fire, figuring my options.

Not many.

None good.

My biggest problem was time. The sky had begun to pale ever so slightly in the east, and since the moon had already passed overhead that could mean only one thing—dawn.

Sunrise is about five A.M. at midsummer. From the sky, it was probably an hour away—hour and a half at the best.

Power had said twelve hours—seven o'clock, or close to it. If he was earnest about facing financial ruin after that hour, what did he have to lose by hurting Maria? Maybe he would just throw her to Ben and Jerry for scraps.

But for all that, my first priority was sitting across from me, staring into the fire.

If his bosses got back with word that their boy was better, they would dispose of me like fish guts. The alternative was worse.

I'd been tortured before. A long time ago. I would not let it happen again.

Headlights flashed beyond the trees. I heard the crunch of big tires on dirt and rock, and I knew the time had come to make a decision.

Twenty-six

The big man must have anticipated my move, because as I leaned forward, he spoke.

"Don't fuck around."

"No?"

"It'll all be over soon." His eyes never left the fire.

"What," I said, moving forward on my knees, "do you see in there?"

His head jerked up. He stared at me as if he'd been slapped. Stupid bastard, I thought. Just looking at the unthinking eyes brought the anger rushing forward. I let it flow.

There was the enemy. That look. That mindless, arrogant power. The destructive force without reasoned logic, without ethical belief, without depth. There it was. In his face. I lunged forward.

For his size he moved well and quickly. He'd have had me, except he was expecting one thing, and I gave him another. As it was, my move worked by the narrowest of margins.

As I dove forward with my hands in front of me, he rocked forward to meet me. His hands came up to defend the blow, his muscular legs planted in the dirt.

But when he clapped his hands together, he was grabbing at air. I was ducking below.

Suddenly he was off balance. Having set for the impact, he was leaning too far forward, his weight held up by nothing, his feet digging hard, like a lineman against a practice dummy.

His arms flailed. Then he was falling in on me.

But I had already made my move, suicidal or not. I tucked my right hand down, twisting hard against the duct tape, trying to turn it as far away from my left hand as possible. Even so, I ended up with some burns on the back of my right hand. But they were nothing like the left.

I dug my left hand into the fire, deep into the coals, feeling the heat, like the rage inside, blasting through my skin. I came up with a pile of the red hot embers and, screaming, shot my hand upward in an openhanded uppercut.

The big man, coming down, met the hand halfway, pressing the already searing coals further into my palm.

For all that, he got the worst of the bargain. I ground the coals into his eyes.

Then I was rolling out from under him and he was stumbling forward, blind and in pain, like a wounded bear. He landed on his knees in the fire, rolled away from it, still swatting at his eyes, shaking and twisting in great convulsions, screaming.

I looked back once over my shoulder and I could see his pants on fire, his suit catching. The two men bursting out of the trees toward him.

Then I was gone.

Twenty-seven

I knew they would come after me. How long? Two minutes, three? It wouldn't take much time to dump the big man in the bed of the truck and get moving. Or, if he was as badly hurt as I thought he was, to decide he was of no further use to them. A blind killer is not much of a killer.

As if to confirm the thought, I heard a single gunshot in the darkness behind me.

I ran forward, stumbling over the ground. I tripped over a rock and landed on a yucca plant. Where in the hell was I?

Ahead of me was a hill. I could see the darkened hump of it silhouetted against the stars. This was a rocky slope, with grass and yucca, and sotol poking up like giant cotton swabs.

I struggled up the hill, climbing as quickly as I could, but still feeling sluggish from the knock I'd taken in the head, and hampered by my hands, the one screaming with pain, both still bound together.

I stopped at a large rock, dropped to my knees, leaned against it. I felt sweat, cool and thick on my forehead, and that pain. It throbbed with each heartbeat, an intense fire that covered the palm and most of the fingers of my left hand.

I rubbed the tape back and forth against the rough edge of the rock, felt a little progress. The pain came and I squeezed my eyes closed.

I was still rubbing the tape furiously against the serrated edge of the rock when the manic whine of the truck rose out of the desert behind me and the headlights flashed over a rise, heading my way.

All of a sudden, it was too much. The pain was overwhelming. The lights were bright, the engine roaring, the truck only moments away. It was just too damn much. Too much pain for too long. I felt the anger and the panic draining away, the sluggishness of despair creeping in.

Why? a voice inside asked. Why keep trying? You don't know where you are—the middle of nowhere, anyway—and you are all alone, unarmed. And they are coming. They will find you. Again. And again. Why fight the inevitable?

I looked again at the bright headlights of the truck, the row of daylighters above the windshield had been switched on, and it rushed toward me from the darkness like something out of a Spielberg movie. Beyond, above, came the roar of the jet engines, and—blam blam blam—I squeezed my eyes shut as the shells burst. I opened my eyes and saw that it wasn't bombs, but the echo of gunfire, the hand sticking out the truck window, the black object flashing, then another echoing report.

Why?

Because, I thought, you don't give up. It's not in you. You promised Ryder you would get him home. Until you have done that, your debts aren't paid, and you won't stop until they break you, cut you down, kill you. It will take that much.

I climbed. I glanced back over my shoulder and saw the lights. Apparently a road ran along the base of the hill. I must have missed it when I crossed over it, but I could see it clearly now in the truck's headlights.

I huffed, my breath coming in great gulps as I scrambled up the hill. I looked back again. They had stopped. And then the hand poked out the window again. A beam flicked on, and a searchlight began playing across the hillside.

I turned away, felt the beam on me, saw my shadow in stark contrast on the rocky ground as I scrambled toward the top.

The gunfire erupted in a rapid burst. Then I was over the top and stumbling down the other side.

From the far side, I could see that the road wrapped around the hill, cutting across the desert below me. Beyond that lay the lights of the city, tucked safely in the V where the hills came together. I recognized the view immediately. And as I did, I knew there might be a way out of this. I scrambled down the hill and across the road, knowing just where I was headed.

On the other side of the road, the ground leveled out. I ran a few feet farther, then slowed. I dropped to the ground and found another craggy rock, ran the tape across it, once, twice, then cut through. I pulled my right wrist free, the tape dangling loosely from the left.

The truck rounded the hill, tires slipping in the dirt; then it straightened out. I stood on the flat ground on the far side of the road. The headlights washed over me as the truck pulled through the curve. I stood straight and tall, and I knew they would see me. Then they were jagging off the road, swinging toward me, and I cut and ran.

Ducking low, I sprinted across the flat ground. The headlights came up behind, illuminating the ground around me, and I ran faster, not worrying now about tripping over the rocks.

The beams grew brighter and for a moment I thought I wasn't going to make it, but I glanced back and the truck wasn't as close as I thought, the daylighters creating the illusion.

I leaped over a low ditch and ran across the flat desert. I heard the roar of the engine as the truck bounced through the ditch, coming up out of it fast, landing hard, pedal to the floor.

Then I was at the edge, and I stopped. Turned around. The truck was on me, maybe twenty feet away—the twin silhouettes of driver and passenger just visible beyond the headlights. I threw myself to the side, feeling the rush of air as the knobby tires shot past me.

The motor screamed as the truck left the ground, the tires spinning freely in open space. There was a long pause. Then the scraping, crunching metal sound, like a hundred garbage cans smashed flat. Then nothing.

I crawled to the edge, looked down into the deep, sheer chasm—Seven Falls, the recreational area off Redington Pass, tucked between the Rincons and the Catalinas.

Two hundred and fifty feet below, at the bottom of the craggy cliff, the deep orange glow of the fire grew, the oily black smoke pouring up to the paling sky.

Twenty-eight

It was a couple of miles to where the dirt road turned to pavement, and maybe three more beyond that to the convenience store.

I ran.

My hand screamed at me the whole way—each pumping rush of blood a tortuous experience. It was as if a pulsing bag of pain had been surgically attached to the end of my wrist.

I ran. With her name and her face flashing in my mind. Like a mantra. You can make it, I told myself. You can make it. With time to spare.

I shambled into the convenience store looking like an escapee from hell—half-expecting the clerk to reach for the phone, dial 911 before I made it through the door.

But the guy behind the counter looked at me with sleepy eyes, unimpressed.

"Had a little accident," I said. I was dirty and sweating. My clothes were filthy, ripped rags. I held my burned hand tucked gently under my right arm.

As I walked down one of the aisles, I dug in my jeans pocket. Found cash. A wave of relief washed over me. I was fortunate Martin and the Cobra hadn't emptied my pockets.

I grabbed all three small boxes of sterile gauze from the shelf. Added tape and two tubes of ointment. I took that up to the counter, went back and grabbed two vials of Tylenol, got a bottle of water from the cooler, and returned to the counter.

I handed the clerk the whole wad of cash, and asked him to peel off the bills. He took two tens, rang it up, handed me the change.

"I'm just going to sit on the cement out there and do this," I said, my voice strained. "What I wonder is if you could do me a big favor and call a cab for me."

"No problem."

It was easy as that.

Twenty-nine

he cab driver glanced at me in the rearview mirror as we climbed the twisting brick drive up the hill.

"No offense," he said, "but are you sure this is the right place? I mean, I ain't Melvin, and you ain't Howard. Am I right?"

"You're right—and this is it," I said.

As we wound our way to the top, a car passed us going the other way. It was a new looking sedan—an Oldsmobile or a Plymouth, with a deep blue paint job. The cab driver eased over to the side and let the big car by.

I looked over at man behind the wheel. He had a jowly, red face. He didn't return my gaze—didn't even seem to notice us.

The Cherokee was absent from the driveway and the front door to the house was open. The thin man was standing on the front steps, looking slowly around, a grim look on his face, as if he knew he needed to move, but had no idea which way to go.

His eyes locked on me as I climbed out of the cab. I gave the driver a twenty and asked him to wait.

"Need to see Power," I said as I approached the thin man.

He nodded back toward the open door without a word. I stepped over the threshold and made my way through the hallways to the office.

The door was open, but I stood there for a moment before entering.

Power was sitting at his huge desk, the shoulders sloped, the head fallen. He had a small book in front of him. After a moment he turned the page.

"Where is she?" I said.

"She?" He said, finally looking up.

"Maria. Don't play games, old man. I told you, if you hurt her I would—"

"She's gone" he said, with a careless wave of his spindly hand.

I moved in on him. My face must have been a mask of fury, but he showed no concern. The hollow look on his face said it all. He was beyond caring.

"Home, she has gone home," he said quietly.

I stopped.

"Please," he said, indicating the phone at one end of the desk.

I picked it up and dialed. She answered on the third ring.

"Yes?" A touch of wariness there.

"Maria?"

"Gray, are you all right, where are you, where have you been, do you need help?"

"Fine," I said. "More or less. I'm in the foothills. How I got here is a long story, and no, I don't think I need any help."

"You answered all of them."

"I'm a slow learner, but when I get hold of something, I'm like a Gila monster."

She sighed. "I'm tired, Gray."

"Did they hurt you?"

"No . . . Gray, what's this all about?"

"I'll be there soon," I said.

"And you'll tell me then."

"Sure."

"Be careful."

"Sure."

I hung up and turned to the old man. He was still reading. He closed the thin book and tossed it down on the desk. I looked at the cover—it was the Hemingway book, *Father Saint.*

"It's gone, Mister Napoleon, it's all gone."

"Gone?"

"Gone. I had Ben and Jerry take your lawyer home, and that is the last work they will do for me."

"Fired them?"

He chuckled humorlessly.

"It is all gone. My financial situation, you see, was much more precarious even than I let on. All of my real assets were being used to support paper wealth. A house of cards. The gems were my last hope. I was after them not only to add to my collection—I needed them to prop up my falling house. I had an appraiser here, ready to authenticate should any of my people find them. Now it is too late. I sent him away."

"What about this place—the paintings, the rugs? It must be worth a fortune."

"Gone. All of it. My wealth has been shrinking for years. I am not nearly as rich as I'm rumored to be. Las Estrellas were my last chance. Within an hour of the opening of the business day in New York—several hours sooner than I expected, actually—I was broke. You see, Mister Napoleon, when you are truly rich, over the years you attract the attention of many unsavory individuals—they are drawn to you like sharks to chum. And they cruise along, waiting for a chance."

"Dangerous game."

"When I gave Ben and Jerry their leave, I thought they were going to cry. I'm all they've ever had. What will they do?"

I shook my head. The Cobra had told me everything I needed to know. I wasn't really interested in the old man's troubles, and wanted nothing more to do with him. I'd only come here for Maria. I had a taxi waiting.

He picked up the book.

"You know," he said, "they really are awful poems. I should have had him sign the other one . . . it's a much better book."

I passed the thin man again on the way out. He was still standing on the porch, staring off into the distance. I nodded toward the cab.

"Need a ride?"

He just shook his head slowly, quietly, side to side, his gaze never leaving the horizon.

Thirty

I gave the driver directions, and soon we were heading west, under the Interstate, to St. Mary's Hospital. Four hours later I walked back out into the sunshine, a fresh, thick wrap of gauze around my hand, a prescription for Percocet in my pocket.

The doctor had wanted me to stay, at least for one night.

"Can't do it, doc," I said. "I still have all those miles to go before I sleep."

"Well, you really need to stay here overnight. Burns are easily infected."

"Doc," I said. "I don't have health insurance."

End of argument.

After I'd gotten all bandaged up, I took the elevator to the third floor, and went to the station.

The nurse behind the counter had black hair and blue eyes. According to the tag on the shirt pocket, his name was Scott.

"Can I help you?" he asked.

I told him I was curious about the condition of the unknown Frenchman.

"Jean Doe? Are you family?"

"No, just a concerned citizen."

"Oh."

"Actually," I said, sensing resistance, "Katy Crimson called me in here to try to help identify him, and I was curious if he'd gotten any better."

"Katy, huhn? Well, no, to be honest, he really didn't. In fact, he expired last night."

I stopped at a pay phone in the lobby and called Maria. She was still home. She said she'd called her office and told Steve to cancel her appointments. She was taking the day off.

"He was so quiet when I told him," she said. "I thought he'd fainted."

"Have you ever taken a day off before?" I asked.

She thought about it for a moment.

"Not that I remember."

"It grows on you. Take my word for it."

Next I called my friend, Nate. He has an old Land Cruiser much like my own. No one answered at his house, so I looked up the number for the local weekly newspaper where he works, and called him there. When I told him what I wanted, he said sure, and a little while later he was picking me up in front of the hospital.

I rode with him back to *The Weekly*'s dumpy little office building. He climbed out and handed me the keys. I walked around to the driver's side.

His vehicle was filthy. It looked like it had never been cleaned. "You know," I said to him, as I started the four-wheel drive back up, "you really should run this thing through the car wash once in a while."

"What for?" he said. Then he turned and walked away.

I drove west, following the curving road along the base of the mountain—Shuk Son, the O'odham called it, giving the city its name.

At Mission Road I headed south, to Ajo Way.

My hand was throbbing, but not as badly as earlier. The Tylenol I'd taken had done a passable job. I would only fill the prescription if I really needed it.

I turned right on Ajo, driving out past Three Points and Sells.

In a couple of hours I was at Why. I pulled in at the gas station, filled the tank, and bought five gallons of drinking water.

The tough-looking man was sitting in the shade in front of the building, leaning back against the wall in his wooden chair just like last time. I looked at him as I walked back out, but his eyes were closed.

I got in the Land Cruiser, opened one of the water jugs. I lifted it and took long deep gulps of the fresh, cool, clean water.

New sweat broke out on my skin. The pump was primed. I lifted the bottle again, and when I had drunk more than half, I stopped. Capped it, set it on the floor by the passenger seat.

I looked over, and the tough-looking man was staring at me. I nodded. He closed his eyes.

Back on the road, I headed northwest. It was the only direction the Frenchman could have gone, since they said he came out of the desert on I-8. A few hundred yards along, I passed a pay phone, planted in the ground next to a saguaro. I watched carefully as I drove, hawking the left side of the road for the clump of crosses.

By the time I got to Ajo, my hopes were falling. Surely it had to have been before then. He wouldn't have gone all the way into town, would he? Too risky.

I pulled over to the side. Stopped. I lifted the bottle from the floor and drank again. The water was already lukewarm, the metal floor of the Land Cruiser heating it quickly under the blistering sun.

It had to be a hundred and fifteen degrees. Maybe more. The kind of weather that breaks a man. Sends him home.

I turned around, and headed back the way I came. When I got to the gas station I turned around, and drove slowly up toward Ajo again.

This time I counted. One cross, two . . .

When I got to five, I slowed to a crawl. And then I saw it. The thin tracks of a jeep trail, cutting off the road to the left, heading out toward the gunnery range.

I pulled off the highway, stopped for a moment, contemplating the road ahead of me—certain now of what I would find there.

Then I eased forward, crawling down the rough dirt trail at a moderate speed. After a few hundred yards the road turned bad. It went through a series of twists and turns, doubling back on itself a couple of times.

Then began a series of deep dips and climbs. I dropped into one, started up the other side, felt the tires slipping, and hit the brakes.

I climbed out and locked the hubs, then dropped the vehicle into four-wheel low. It crawled easily up the steep hill.

I crested the peak and had started down the far side when I saw the truck. It was in a wash—wider than the rest, the sand deeper.

He had gotten stuck trying to turn around. The back wheels were dug into the sand. It was clear from the marks that he did not have four-wheel drive. He'd scooped some of the sand away, then apparently given up, and begun to walk.

The box was in the bed of the truck, and as I pulled up to it, I saw how easy it must have been. The tailgate of the truck bed and that of the Land Cruiser were the same height. It would have been no problem to back up to the bed of the Land Cruiser, hop out, jump up there and shove the box up onto the lip. Once you got it halfway, you could tilt it, and let gravity do the work.

I climbed out and walked around to the truck. His error had been in trying to turn around in the sand. Big mistake.

He had come to a stop under the branches of a large palo verde, and the truck, I figured, would be invisible from the air.

The smell was bad, and that's all I'll say about it. The coffin had been opened, and the lid was resting loosely on top of it. I pushed it aside, and looked in. Nothing I want to talk about. But the calendar stick was gone.

I climbed back in and swung around, backing up to the bed of the truck. I climbed out, found a good sized flat stone, and hopped in next to the box. I pushed the lid into place, and nailed it shut, using the stone as a hammer. Then I grabbed the end of the box with my good hand, and pulled. Moved it a foot, then two, then got behind and pushed with my legs. It slid up to the halfway point, then tilted, and slid down into the Land Cruiser.

Nothing to it. The whole operation took maybe two minutes. The Frenchman had plenty of time.

I would never know exactly how it went down, but the Frenchman and Caroline, or Julia, if that was her name, must have been working together. Maybe they really were brother and sister. Probably she left for Tucson ahead of him, intending to be there if he failed and the body made it to Ryder's family. He must have been waiting at the morgue, and followed me out of there. At Why, he saw his opportunity and took advantage of it.

I had no idea why he had driven so far down this dirt road. It is strange that way. You start down a dirt road into the desert, not knowing where, or how far you're going. And you are drawn away, out there, into it. Hours later you pause, wiping the sweat off your forehead, and you realize your hands and arms are shaking and weak, exhausted from fighting the wheel.

By the time he realized he'd gone far enough, he'd gone a little too far.

His big error, though, hadn't been getting stuck. His big mistake had come afterward. When he walked away.

If he'd stayed on the road, and followed it back to the highway, he would have been all right. But he had decided to cut across the desert, take a shortcut, and avoid the long, twisting road.

Out there in the desert, it is easy to get turned around, lost. It happens all the time. You read about the worst cases in the paper. He had lost his bearings, and soon he was started on the forced march. How he had made it across the fifty miles to the highway, I would never know. It was quite a feat. One hell of a walk. Some kind of record, maybe.

After I had the box settled into place, I sat down on the ground on the shaded side of the Land Cruiser, leaning back against the rear wheel. I pulled the water bottle down, uncapped it, and chugged it empty. I tossed the container back into the jeep.

I was sweating hard, the trembling feel of heat all over me. I rested for a while.

Then I got up and walked over to the truck. I looked inside the cab. Empty. I walked around the front. The footprints started on the other side. They led roughly southwest down the wash. I followed the footprints, walking about a hundred yards down the wash. Where the wash jagged right, he had turned up onto the low bank. Here the ground was hard, and the footprints disappeared.

I walked on, cutting for sign through the bushes. I was just about to give up and turn back when I found the calendar stick—broken in half, lying at the foot of an organ pipe cactus.

I picked it up and looked inside. Empty. I dropped the pieces of wood where I'd found them, turned, and walked away.

Thirty-one

I am climbing a steep slope on the face of Baboqui-
vari. Nate is above me, covering ground with his cus-
tomary athletic ease.
We are visiting I'itoi's cave. It is here that the Life
Giver settled to live out eternity underground after
giving life to first man and first woman.
Ryder is below, showing us the way. He is speaking
O'odham—the words, the sounds are not from this
time; they are from long ago, they are from before.
Nate reaches the cave first. I see him pause, then duck
inside. Just for a moment, then he is backing away.
When he scrambles back down the hill toward me he
is no longer wearing his belt. He is smiling.
I claw my way up the steep slope—all toes and
hands, loose dirt skittering—then I am there. Maybe
it is the heat of the day, maybe it is fatigue, but the
energy of things seems to have climbed a notch. As I
duck into the cave I expect to sense in the background
a steady thrumming—as if here, at the center of the
universe, I will be so close to the source of the power
of life that I will hear its deep rumble.
But the cave is dead quiet. Ryder's voice slips away as
I step inside and my ears are filled with the soft,
musty silence of rock.
Bits of string hang from the ceiling, candles line the
walls—little offerings to I'itoi. This is the tradition. I
see Nate's belt, coiled like a docile serpent where he
left it near the entrance.
I kneel down. Breathe in the dank air. Listen for a
memory. Nothing.
I can think of nothing to leave. All my gear is in the
truck. I pat my shirt pockets, taking inventory, and

something jangles. I reach under the shirt with one hand, feel the ridges stamped in the little metal rectangles. I grab the thin chain with both hands and pull the dog tags over my head. I run my hand along the wall and find a small notch in the protruding rock. Hanging from it is a small key on a piece of string, above that a dried out ocotillo flower secured by a twist tie. I have been wearing the dog tags for seventeen years. I hook them over the rock, then turn and stumble out, quickly before I change my mind.

As I step into the sunlight, I squint, blinded by the glare. I feel the smile on my lips, the hot sun on my face. Ryder's voice floats up to me from below like a good smell—fresh bread, mesquite smoke, rain. He is laughing, laughing.

I left early in the morning for the funeral.

With the sun rising behind me, I made my way out to the rez, and then down the bumpy road to Joaquin ki.

Uncle Charlie came out to greet me as I pulled up, and as I walked with him to the house, he put an arm around my shoulder.

"Hey," he said. "I just want to say again . . . thanks."

"He was a friend," I said. "Can't leave a friend behind."

"You know, maybe you're okay."

"Think so?"

"Well . . . maybe," and we both laughed.

In the front room of the little adobe house, there was a festive atmosphere. People talked and laughed, some of the men telling long stories in the soft language of the People. There was plenty to eat and drink—red chile and beef-bone stew, flour tortillas and beans and vegetable stew, coffee and red Koolaid to wash it down. A band of O'odham musicians had set up under the ramada, and they were playing traditional Waila tunes.

Theresa Joaquin saw me duck through the low doorway, and she broke away from a group sitting around the table.

She thanked me, and again I said it hadn't really been that bad.

The back room of the house was dark, and people filed through the doorway to the coffin, looking in on Ryder, paying respects.

After the funeral, that room would be torn down, the walls burned, the doorway sealed.

I waited until things were quiet, and when I walked into the room, I was alone.

I went halfway to the casket and stopped. That was as far as the customs of my people allowed—like Navajos, we WASPs don't deal all that well with corpses.

I stood there in the cool, quiet room for a while, thinking.

After loading the box I had headed back toward Tucson. I stopped at Sells and called the Ajo sheriff's office. Cavroni, much to my surprise, was in, and I talked to him for a few minutes, explaining that I had found the body I'd lost, along with the truck of the person who stole it, and I wanted to do things right.

A couple of hours later, having first directed me to take the body to the only undertaker in Sells, he finished taking my statement at tribal headquarters. A tribal police officer was there, too, and he asked questions as I explained what had happened.

Leaving out the part about Power, and Marsted and the Cobra, I told them about the phone call from the hospital, the visit to the dying man, the drive in the desert.

Cavroni eyed me suspiciously the whole time, but finally, after consulting with the O'odham officer, he let me go.

Afterward, I drove straight to the Joaquin ki with the news.

There was still something bothering me. Why had the Frenchman been saying my name? How had he known to contact me?

The answer, of course, was waiting for me at home. And had been all along.

I walked in the door tired, hot, my left hand a pulsing lump of pain.

I found a plastic bag, thought about pulling it over my head, but stuffed my hand in it instead, slipped a rubber band over that, and took a long, relaxing shower.

When I got out, I wrapped a towel around my waist, walked over to the box, started to put on a CD, but thought better of it.

What I needed was silence. Clear, cool silence.

I turned the swamp cooler on high, flopped onto the bed. I tried to sleep. But something was bugging me. Something in the back of my mind. A tiny, unscratched itch.

Finally it went away, and I slipped into sleep.

In the dream I was running. Running with the bombs falling all around me, the jets roaring overhead. I broke out of the jungle, into a clearing and found . . . a wall. A wall? A huge red wall. And back in there somewhere, a light blinking. I held up a hand. The light blinked. And each pulse of bright red light brought with it a flash of pain. Pain that started in my . . .

I woke up, realized I was lying on my hand, and rolled over, freeing it. Held it out at my side. The pain was coming fresh and strong now, shooting up my arm with each heartbeat. No way I could get back to sleep.

I got up, walked across the room, found shorts and a T-shirt, pulled them on. I crossed to the answering machine. The display was blinking 5. I pressed the button, listened to the whir as the tape rewound, then clicked and started forward.

The first message was a familiar voice, though sounding a lot better than the last time I'd heard it—the only time I'd heard it—the accent thick and rich, and I listened to half of it before stopping the tape and rewinding it. Then I sat on the floor with my head next to the machine and listened all the way through.

"Monsieur Napoleon, you do not know me, but I have been following you," the Frenchman said. "I am now at the telephone a short distance to the north of someplace called Why? I have taken your name and phone number from a piece of paper attached to a box— a box I believe you will be wanting back. I do not wish to keep it, only to borrow it a short time. I will leave it in a safe place in the desert, then call you again to instruct you where to find it. I apologize for the inconvenience, but I'm afraid it is necessary. *Bon soir.*"

Click.

I sat there for a long time thinking—I gotta quit letting things pile up.

The next day, I picked up my Land Cruiser at the wrecking yard where the cops had towed it. The roll bar was tweaked, and the front window smashed. I pushed the window frame forward, locking it to the hood. I would have to wear a pair of sunglasses when I drove, but it was better than nothing. There was a lot of paperwork to deal with—a desert of bureaucracy to walk across—but finally I left in possession of my vehicle, $110 poorer.

Now, two days later, I stood in the dark room, looking at the new coffin that held Ryder Joaquin's body.

"Rest easy," I said finally, quietly, and I turned away.

Half an hour later, the coffin was loaded onto the back of a pickup, and everybody piled into vehicles for the drive to the village.

The hole had been dug in a graveyard next to the small chapel. The casket was pulled from the back of the truck, and set by the hole. I noticed that someone had placed a crucifix on top of the casket.

A priest had come from Covered Wells and he said a prayer over the coffin. When he was done he took the crucifix from the casket and handed it to Theresa Joaquin. Then, starting with Theresa Joaquin and Uncle Charlie, one by one the People passed by the casket again as they had done at the ki.

Then the casket was lowered into the hole with ropes.

The hole itself had been dug on the east-west axis, and the coffin was placed with the head at the west end—finally Ryder would be able to face east and watch the rising sun. The hole had been dug with a shelf on each side, just above the height of the casket. If you had stood in the grave, at the end of the casket, and looked forward, you would have seen an odd T shape. After the ropes were pulled away, wooden slats were lowered down, rested on the shelves, side to side above the coffin. Then a thick cotton blanket was lowered onto the slats, covering the whole thing.

One by one, the People walked to the side of the grave and dropped in a handful of sand. I took my place at the back of the line, shuffled forward, and did the same.

Then a few men grabbed shovels, and filled the rest of it in.

After the grave was covered the women knelt down and decorated it with candles and flowers. Then they stood up, and Theresa moved over by Uncle Charlie. They stood next to the grave as everyone present walked by and shook their hands.

Again I took my place at the end of the line. When I took Theresa

Joaquin's hand, she squeezed gently. I looked into her eyes, and she smiled, a quiet, sad smile.

As I was leaving, Charlie walked up behind me, grabbed me by the elbow.

"Hey, Napoleon," he said. "Come here. Someone I want you to meet."

We walked over to the chapel where a stocky young man was sitting in the shade. He stood as we approached.

"Hey," Uncle Charlie said, "this is him."

The young man nodded quietly.

"Sandy Asoza," he said.

I offered a hand. His grip was gentle.

"I'm Gray Napoleon."

"Yeah."

We were all quiet for a little while.

"Listen," Sandy said finally, "thanks for what you did."

"Sure," I said. "Can I ask you a question?"

He looked at Charlie, then back at me, then away.

"Sure."

"When you went down to your grandparents' place, you were running from them?"

He nodded.

"Ryder told you he was taking the calendar stick, and then later the French girl told you how much trouble he was in, she was in—maybe you were in?"

Again, the nod.

"So you holed up at your grandparents', and camped out, in case they found out where you were and came after you—thinking you and Ryder were in on it together?"

"It's a great view from up there," he said. "You can see everything."

"Your grandparents—they know you're okay?"

"I stayed there last night."

"When we went down there," I said, "I climbed up to Ho'ok ki. Saw where you camped. Saw the pattern you drew on the rocks. Why'd you do that?"

He considered the question for a while.

In the end he said, "I had a lot of time on my hands." Then he paused. Finally, "I guess I was making a trail of the diamonds. Leading to Ho'ok ki. So maybe those men who were after them, the ones who were chasing Ryder, maybe they'd run into Ho'ok instead."

Thirty-two

My mistake was stopping at Nacho's. But it was hot, the sun beating down on me like I was its stepchild, and I thought just one beer would cut the glare.

I pulled into the mostly empty lot, parked, and walked inside.

There were only two patrons at the bar—young O'odham men. They looked familiar, but I couldn't really place them. They were sitting in the booth by the jukebox, but no music was playing.

I sat down at the bar, and the bartender walked over, his perfect silver helmet of hair shimmering above him.

He looked at me with eyebrows raised.

"Beer," I said, and named my brand.

He turned to the old, rusty cooler, pulled out a bottle, opened it, and set it on a napkin in front of me.

I put down a five and he took it. Made change. I let it ride.

In the weeks since the funeral my burns had healed, and I lifted the drink with my left hand, testing the grip.

I had just about finished when the door opened and daylight flashed in.

I watched the silhouettes as they rumbled across the threshold. One, two, three. Big, familiar shapes.

As the door swung closed, I made their features. Ugly. The one with the huge belly smiling like a fat wolf.

Shit, I thought. This is it. They're going to kill me.

They stood by the door, letting their eyes adjust. Then they walked over to me, standing in a loose circle, keeping a few feet away.

The two guys by the jukebox got up quietly and left.

"But oh, my shithead," the belly said. "Thy time has come."

I spun around on the bar stool. The three of them took a step back. The belly was wearing a leather vest over his dirty T-shirt, and he pulled it back, showing me the pistol holstered underneath. Big bastard. .357.

"Let's take a walk."

"Hell," I said.

"Yeah," he said. "You bet."

His two partners moved in on me from the sides, grabbed my shoulders. I didn't resist. The gun made the odds way too long. If they were going to kill me, I wanted to delay the moment as long as possible. I didn't see any percentage in forcing them to shoot me right here.

They dragged me from the stool, started walking me toward the door. I stayed up, walked under my own power.

We were halfway to the door when it was pushed open from the outside. One of the two men who'd just left stepped in. Followed by another. And another.

I heard a little shout from outside, and the sound of car doors slamming. Two more of the men came in. They had rifles slung jauntily across their shoulders, like extras in a Western.

The big Indian spoke. "You're a little ways out of your neighborhood," he said to the belly.

"What the hell is it to you?"

"Whatever you want it to be."

"I don't want it to be nothin'. Me and my boys was just leaving."

"That's fine," the big man said, his eyes twinkling. And he stepped aside.

The belly started forward, and I felt the other two pulling at my shoulders. I dug in with my heels, about to take my best shot.

It didn't matter. The O'odham put his hand out as the big man stepped forward, stopping him.

"Thing is, I was going to have a beer with my cousin, here," he nodded in my direction, "and it looks like you're trying to take him with you." He spoke to me, "Unless you *want* to go?"

"A beer sounds good," I said.

"Who the hell you think you are?" the big man asked.

"The question is, who in the hell do you think *you* are?"

One of the belly's partners made a move, and the rifles dropped down to waist level.

"Easy," the belly said.

"I mean, you come out here to the rez, try to kidnap one of my relatives—"

"Reservation don't start for three miles," the belly said.

The big Indian looked around at his partners.

"Where's the rez start?" he asked.

"Starts right here," one said.

"Yeah," someone agreed.

"Starts at the Tucson city limits."

"Starts in New York."

"Looks like you were wrong."

The belly thought about it for a moment.

"Yeah," he finally said, his face flushed, forehead beaded with sweat from the burning indigestion of swallowed anger. "Maybe I made a mistake."

"Be a bigger mistake if you come back, kimosabe," the big Indian said, and he stepped aside. "We see you again, we have to give you a little kimo-therapy."

My new friends laughed as the bikers walked out the door.

In a moment the sound of motors sifted in from the parking lot as they started up their Harleys and roared away.

I still felt shaky inside. The one who'd done the talking patted me on the shoulder. The rest were laughing, and jawing, and now they shuffled past me.

"Hey," the big man said to the ones bellying up to the bar. "No beers. We gotta go to work."

There was some groaning and protest, but they headed back out the door.

I stepped out into the sunlight with him.

"I guess that's the second time we saved your ass," he said.

"Thanks, I—second time?"

"You wouldn't know. But who do you think stopped them from killing you before?"

I remembered the three men at the end of the bar, the quiet looks, the fight with the bikers, then running for the door. I had wondered why the bikers hadn't done more damage when they had the chance. Now I knew.

"I remembered you from back when you came out to Vaya Chin with Ryder a few years back—that's where my parents live, Vaya Chin."

"Years ago," I said. "I remember."

"We followed you over to the Joaquin place, too, just to make sure you made it there all right."

I remembered the truck pulling up to the ki in the night, Theresa Joaquin going out to greet it, talking to the people inside.

I shook my head, smiling in disbelief.

The men piled into a shiny new, blue GMC truck.

"Well, what can I say, but thanks."

"You know," he said, "it looks to me like maybe you enjoy doing things the hard way. You ought to take it easy. You ever think about that?"

I nodded, laughed, thanked him again.

"You don't owe us any thanks," he said. "I went to school with Ryder . . . when we were kids. He was two years older than me. I always looked up to him." He paused. "It's good he made it home."

He turned toward the truck.

"I gotta go," he said. "Gotta get to work."

"Work?"

"Casino of the Sun. Indian gaming hall." He climbed behind the wheel of the truck. "Custer is a little old lady from Iowa," he said, as he started the motor and dropped it into reverse. "And Little Bighorn is a dollar slot."

Thirty-three

I am walking in the desert with Ryder Joaquin. Just
walking . . .

I told myself I didn't really know where I was headed. I just needed to get away. Out there. I needed the desert.

Maria was angry with me again, and not taking my calls. She hadn't expressed any interest in going to Ryder's funeral, so I went alone. Now she was pissed at me for not taking her along. I didn't really understand why she was upset, but I figured she would get over it. Maybe.

I headed west on 86, and a couple of hours later I drove past the gas station at Why. I turned right, toward Ajo.

I found myself watching the crosses, and soon I came to the turnoff. I pulled over to the side, sat for a while, looking up the thin dirt trail. Finally I figured what the hell, and I turned off the highway and headed up the jeep track. A few hundred feet along I stopped the Land Cruiser and got out, locking the hubs. I climbed back in and dropped it into four-wheel drive. Why wait?

Soon I came to the spot where the Frenchman had gotten stuck. Apparently the sheriff's deputies had already been there, since the vehicle was gone.

I stopped under the huge palo verde where the truck had sat. It seemed as good a place as any.

I switched off the engine and climbed out, hauling my pack out of the bed.

It was big and heavy—three gallons of water and four days' supply of freeze-dried food. I hefted it onto my back.

I looked up the wash the way the Frenchman had gone, then turned and looked out at the desert into which he had eventually wandered.

The nurse had said he walked out of the desert on I-8. I'd checked with the sheriff's department, and they told me he'd been found near a junction called Sentinel. North by northwest.

In that direction lay Abbey's Air Force bombing range. I wondered how long the Frenchman had walked before he finally dropped the gems. A day? Maybe two? Hard to say.

When you are finally convinced that your death is imminent, nothing else matters. Certainly not money, or precious rocks. And wandering through the desert dehydrated, every extra weight becomes an unbearable burden.

Not such a bad thing, really. Suddenly what is truly important becomes clear. You simply want to continue. Walking. Living.

I calculated roughly. To be certain of covering the ground the Frenchman had walked, you would have to head north, cutting for sign over an area twenty miles wide, fifty miles long. Through rock and scrub and cactus, with nothing for company but a few Air Force targets, and no sound but the occasional explosions of a bombing run. To complicate matters, the monsoons were coming. Soon the desert would be deluged for a few hours every afternoon. Things have a way of slipping down into the mud. Disappearing. If he got lucky, and he didn't get blown up, a man could spend his whole life out there, looking. And still not find the gems. Still not touch Las Estrellas.

To the south, opposite the direction the Frenchman had gone, lay the Growler Mountains, the wildlife refuge at Cabeza Prieta, and beyond that, Organ Pipe Cactus National Monument. A lot of beautiful, empty desert that way.

I turned south. And I walked.